GHOST SONG

SUSAN PRICE

Ghost Song

FARRAR STRAUS GIROUX

NEW YORK

To my mother and father.
About time.

GHOST SONG

1

In a place far distant from where you are now grows an oak-tree by a lake.

Round the oak's trunk is a chain of golden links.

Tethered to the chain is a learned cat, and this most learned of all cats walks round and round the tree continually.

As it walks one way, it sings songs.

As it walks the other, it tells stories.

This is one of the stories the cat tells.

I tell (says the cat) of a far-distant, northern Czardom, where half the year is summer and light, and half the year is winter dark.

I tell of the strangeness of summer and winter and the earth's turning. Summer so short, and yet its days so long: one bright day pours endlessly into another and the sun shines at midnight.

But winter so long, and its days shorten and shorten until noon is dark, and above the snow-covered land the freezing black sky presses down, heavy with the thousands of sharp, glittering stars and the white, white moon.

The story I tell begins (says the cat) in these cold wastes where the moonlight rises from the snow and half-melts the darkness to a silver mist. It begins with the

1

lonely hunter Malyuta journeying over the snow to look at his traps.

On his left foot was strapped a long ski; on his right foot a short ski, and in his gloved hand he carried a bow, with which he pushed himself along in a fast glide. The wind flung ice crystals in his face, and shook the edge of his big, furred hood with a groan, and, listening to that sad, sad sound, Malyuta thought back across the miles to the village he had left, to his friends and his wife. They had certainly forgotten him, he thought. In that cold and emptiness he found it hard to remember himself. He felt that he was a ghost, already dead and blowing through endless cold and darkness in the wind's voice.

Some men could stay warm by the stove through the winter months, but not Malyuta. He was a slave of the Czar – though he had never seen him – and a Czar needs furs. A Czar needs the soft black furs of sables, and the spotted soft whiteness of ermine; a Czar needs wolf-skins and lynx-skins, and beaver fur to line his cloak and slippers. He needs these skins so that he can dress himself in them and feel himself to be a true Czar; he needs them to give as presents to others so that others, too, will believe him a true Czar.

And because of this need, Malyuta had to leave his family every winter to hunt these animals, trap them and kill them and tear off their skins. He was a huntsman of the Czar.

It happened (says the cat) that, in one of his traps, he found a dead sable. He took off his skis and knelt in the snow, looking down at the hard, stiff, frozen little body, lying twisted, as it had died, with a tight noose about its neck. He saw how intensely black was its fur against the glimmering snow, and how – even in the poor light – the scarlet of its blood flared against the white snow and its own black fur. 'My first son . . .' said Malyuta, through his heavy, ice-hung beard. Soon he hoped to have a son. '. . . So should my first son be – black, black hair; black like his mother's hair, black like the sable's fur. White skin, white teeth, white like the snow. Red lips, red cheeks, red as the blood in them, red as the blood in the snow . . . Black, white and red; sable, snow and blood.'

He spoke his wish aloud – spoke it there, in that cold, dark, shimmering emptiness, where the wind could carry his words for ever. He spoke his wish above the body of a sable that had died in his traps, but he spoke no words to soothe its angry ghost – angry, unappeased, hungry as sables always are.

It is never wise to speak a wish aloud, but to speak it in such a place, in such company – that is to ask misery to live with you.

But whatever misery people wish on themselves, the earth still turns and, as it turns, the days grow longer and the nights shorter. When the long winter night began to be broken by short, dim days, Malyuta loaded his sled with his tent and his frozen skins. He harnessed his reindeer to the sled and, with his shaggy, blue-eyed dogs running alongside, he drove over the snow to the city and the Czar's storehouse. Only after he had delivered the furs, and had been given his reward in food and cloth, was he free to return home.

Malyuta ran alongside the sled with the dogs rather than slow the reindeer with his weight. He helped the reindeer pull the sled over the thawing snow. Quicker, quicker! His mind and his heart were full of Yefrosinia, who had been his wife for only a year.

Malyuta was not young or handsome and, being a slave, he was a poor man. And so for a long time he had not married, nor had any home of his own. He had spent his winters alone, and the short summers lodging in the villages owned by the Czar where, as one of the Czar's huntsmen, he could demand shelter. But for many, many years he had wanted a wife, and children. What is a huntsman without a wife? When he goes away into the winter darkness, who is there to remember him if he has no wife? Who is there to call him back into the firelight of the house, back to summer, once more? And if a slave has no children, what is he? A slave's only riches are his children.

But Malyuta had never had the courage to ask a woman to marry him until he saw Yefrosinia. He was not young, and nor was she. He was not handsome, and she was not pretty. He had nothing and she, being the plain, eldest daughter of a slave who worked the Czar's land, had still less. So he had asked her to be his wife, and she had gladly said yes.

And when Malyuta's sled was dragged into the street of the village, over the last of the melting snow, Yefrosinia was waiting for him, wrapped in a big shawl. Whatever beauty Yefrosinia had – in the darkness of her long hair, in her dark eyes – Malyuta saw it as she stood there in the snow. And when she saw Malyuta, his broad square head fringed round with thick, fair beard and thick, curling hair, she thought he looked more like a shaggy square-headed terrier than ever. He should bark, she thought, as he came up to her.

'I have good news for you, my old dog,' she said, tugging his beard. 'I am going to have a child.'

Malyuta hugged her tightly, and kissed her and, that

4

night, got very, very drunk, to celebrate both his home-coming and the child to come – who, he was sure, would be a son: a black, red and white son.

Summer came, short and hot. The sun's heat lovingly stroked the skin. Children ran naked in the village's dusty streets, and dogs lay panting, and cats lay basking. Women left off their shawls and stockings. Men stripped off their shirts, and the sun drew water out of their skins as they worked and burned them to leather.

Knowing the time to be short, grass, bright, bright green, sprang from the earth. The trees foamed with blossom and were buzzed through by bees. Flowers spread their petals beside every path, beside every stream, even on the roofs of the houses. In the fields vegetables spurted green leaves and rye grew bearded. Sheep lambed, cows calved, birds nested and laid. In the streams small fish teemed. In all this heat and life no one, not even Malyuta, could remember how cold, how dark, how barren, winter was.

And then the child of Yefrosinia and Malyuta was born – at midnight, in the first moments of Mid-summer's Day, which is the longest day of the whole year, the day when there is no second of darkness.

The men of the house were made to sit outside, in the white night, while the baby was being born. They sat on the wooden bench that ran along the front of the hut, and drank, and laughed, and those with children told stories of their children's birth and babyhood. Malyuta sat among them, blushing, proud that he was soon to be a father at last, but afraid that something terrible would happen: that Yefrosinia or the baby would die.

When a smiling woman came to the door to call the men in, Malyuta was the first on his feet and the first into

5

the house. He went straight to the bed, smiling a huge, foolish, tearful grin as soon as he saw that Yefrosinia was well and was smiling back at him. He lowered his weight carefully on to the bed, afraid of hurting her, and kissed her, in love and gratitude.

Yefrosinia's mother came near, with the newborn baby in her arms, and offered it to Malyuta. 'A son,' she said, and Malyuta goggled at her.

Trembling with all the joy and fear and wonder that he felt, Malyuta took the baby in his arms. His son had an ugly red face and a fuzz of black hair on the top of his head. Gently, very gently and carefully, Malyuta lowered his big clumsy head and kissed the baby's forehead. His beard prickled its face and made it cry, and everyone else laughed aloud – a great noise in the wooden house.

Startled by the laughter, Malyuta looked up, with tears in his eyes. Then he laughed himself, and laid the baby beside his wife. He held her hand and looked at her, unable to speak, and shaking his head continually as the tears ran down his face. And she smiled too, tired though she was, to see her big old terrier so happy.

A slave's children are his only wealth. Well, now, Malyuta thought, he had the first coin in his purse.

It was midsummer and there was no darkness to send the people to bed. They began to celebrate the baby's birth. They fetched wooden cups and plates, poured beer, fetched neighbours, and the neighbours came carrying food with them. There was eating and drinking, and many toasts to Yefrosinia, to Malyuta, and to the new little boy. Malyuta carried the baby around to everyone, his face red with pride at being a father at long last, when he had begun to think that he would die without a son to leave in the world behind him.

So Midsummer's Day passed; and the evening, when it came, was as bright as the morning. When the people, tired out, wanted to go to bed and sleep, they had to cover the windows with shutters to make it dark inside their houses.

Soon only Malyuta was left awake. Despite all that he had drunk, he couldn't sleep. He was too excited, and too afraid.

It was dark inside the house, but the summer light shone through the cracks around the shutters in long, dust-shimmering beams of white light that made the shadows darker. It was hot, too, and the heat brought the scent out of the wooden walls, and added it to the heavy scent of beer and food.

Malyuta sat on the edge of his wife's bed and watched her and the baby sleep. His thickly hairy legs were bare, because he had taken off his clothes, ready for bed, even though he had no wish to sleep, and he was dressed only in his shirt. He was thinking long, muddled thoughts. Again and again he bent low over the baby, holding his own breath, to make sure that his son still breathed. He could not believe that something so tiny and new could breathe all by itself.

I now have all I have ever wanted, he said to himself, and the thought stunned him, and made him afraid. I am no longer the traveller who comes to stay in the village, the lonely man. Now I, too, have a wife, and a son. I belong here: this is my village because it is my wife's village and the place where my son was born. And what a son he is and will be! Already he has black hair. Black, white and red he'll be: sable, snow and blood – how can he help but be a great hunter? He'll be handsomer than I ever was and all the women will be eyeing him. I'll teach him how to make a living even when the snow is five feet deep. And when I have to leave this world, I'll leave him behind me, filling my place and his own. 'Ah, your old grandad,' he'll say to his own children. 'Old Malyuta, he was a one!'

Again he bent to make sure that the baby was breathing. He looked at his son's little body, no longer from head to foot than his own forearm. And the baby's small mouth and nose, that breathed for him just as well as Malyuta's great gape and hooter; his little closed eyes. His tiny hands and – smaller and smaller – his tiny fingers, each with a tiny, perfect nail. And this smallness would grow to Malyuta's size!

Now I believe what they say in the churches, Malyuta thought. I believe that water was turned into wine, and that three loaves and five fishes fed ten thousand. If a wonder like this boy of mine can come from two plain folk like my wife and me, then I believe that miracles are true.

He jumped then, for a blow was struck against the outer door of the house, as if the wooden door had been struck with the end of a heavy stick. The dull noise quivered between the wooden house walls, and Malyuta got up angrily from the bed, thinking that the noise would wake his wife and baby. But none of the sleepers in the house stirred at the noise, not even when a second and a third blow were struck before the reverberations of the first had died away.

Malyuta reached for his trousers, and took his long knife from the sheath on his belt before going to the door. It was probably only a neighbour but his love and fear for his wife and new baby made him tender and sore, afraid of every little thing that might threaten them.

He opened the door of the darkened house and was blinded by the white blaze of midsummer midnight. He raised his hand to shelter his eyes and, from behind it, squinted at the man who stood outside – a large man, a dark shape against the brightness. Before Malyuta could think or speak, the man moved forward, and moved so briskly and surely that Malyuta stepped back despite himself and let the stranger into the house. When he quickly turned, his knife ready in his hand, he was blinded by the darkness of the hot, shuttered room.

'Who are you?' Malyuta demanded of the hot darkness. 'What do you want?'

Squinting, he made out the visitor in the middle of the room. The stranger unslung something from his shoulder and dropped it to the floor with a clatter. It was a drum, a flat, oval drum with strange red patterns painted on its skin. Malyuta's heart gave a jolt. It was a ghost-drum; a shaman's drum.

Malyuta walked towards the visitor to get a closer look. His bare, sweaty feet slapped on the wooden floorboards, stuck to them and peeled away with sucking sounds. The stranger stood still, watching Malyuta come, and grinning.

The stranger had a thin, wrinkled face that peered from a thick growth of grey-streaked black hair and beard. His grin showed large white teeth, and crinkled his face into many fine lines. Despite the midsummer heat, he was dressed for winter, as if he had come, in a moment, from the far north where it was still cold. Around his shoulders, in heavy, soft, rank folds, hung the yellow-white skin of a white bear. Its head hung upside-down on the man's shoulders. Its paws, with long black claws, dangled at his sides. Underneath the bearskin cloak the man wore trousers and tunic of reindeer hide, decorated with bones, beads, feathers and brass-rings; and so fantastically embroidered that Malyuta's tired eyes were confused by the many intertwining patterns. On the man's feet were embroidered Lappish boots, and big Lappish mittens were on his hands. A shaman, a night-coming witch – for however brightly the sun shone outside, it was night, white midnight, the last hour of Midsummer's Day.

'I have come for my child,' said the stranger.

'What child?' Malyuta asked, though he both knew and dreaded the answer.

The witch turned towards the bed where Yefrosinia slept, his heavy boots padding softly on the floor like a bear's paws. But Malyuta, with a jump, reached the bed first and took the baby up in his own arms.

'*My* son,' he said. '*My* child.' As he spoke, he looked into the witch's sharp face, and saw the bright sunshine of midnight shining through the still open door, and smelt the scent of grass on the breeze that blew into the house. And he was struck with the certainty that he was dreaming. He had never seen a witch while he was awake. He could give his son to the witch and it wouldn't matter because it was only a dream.

But whenever he had had such frightening dreams before, Malyuta had woken. Could a dream so fill his nostrils with such a rank smell of wild bear? In a dream, would the beams of sunlight be so bright and so hot as they moved over the wrinkles of the witch's face? Would the witch's rough voice buzz so in his ear?

The witch poked his head forward and looked into

Malyuta's face with eyes as black as a bear's. 'My apprentice born. *My* child. Give him to me.'

Malyuta shook his head.

The witch grinned like someone who knows he will have his own way in the end. 'Keep him, and he will be the slave of a Czar. He will labour, and suffer, and in a few years he will die. Give him to me and he will be freer than your Czar. I will teach him the ways to and from the Ghost World and make him a shaman. I will give him three hundred years of life. If it's him that you love, and not yourself, give him to me.'

'No,' said Malyuta.

'Give him to me. You need not fear blame or punishment. I will give you a baby of mud to put in his place, and you can say that the baby died.'

'I don't fear punishment,' Malyuta said. 'I want my son!'

'Women are not so selfish as men. Your wife would give him to me.'

'Let my wife sleep! I am the man, and I have the say. If it is selfish to keep my own son and guard him, then I am selfish! If you want a son, witch, then get your own!'

The witch sighed and turned away from Malyuta to walk towards a wooden bench on the other side of the room. He walked through bright, narrow beams of light, and through deep shadows. His heavy boots padded on the floor, and the bear's claws on them clicked. The edge of the bearskin cloak dragged on the floor with a tiny whispering sound, and a rank bear stink drifted from it to Malyuta's nose. He heard beads and brass-rings rattle on the witch's tunic, and through the open door came the scent of summer flowers and bright white light to drive the shadows into corners.

'The children born of our bodies are not ours,' the witch said. 'Shamans know that. We know that only those reborn from the Ghost World for our teaching are ours, and they may be any man or woman's child . . . In the Ghost World, my friend, grows Iron Wood where all but shamans lose their way . . . And at the centre of Iron Wood grows the Iron Ash. That tree is so big that animals live on its branches, roaming as widely as they do in this world. Those animals feed the shamans who nest in the tree, waiting to be reborn. It was the sables running about the Tree who told me of my apprentice's birth – '

'The sables!' said Malyuta.

The witch nodded. 'That child you hold has been one of us already. He has been reborn to be one of us again. He is my apprentice. I must take him away before the first day of his new life is over. Give him to me.'

A great shock had gone through Malyuta when the witch had spoken of sables. He had remembered kneeling above the dead sable in his trap, and the wish he had spoken then. An even greater dread of the witch came over him. 'No!' he said.

The witch rose angrily from the bench and came towards Malyuta, banging his stick on the floor with a loud noise of wood striking wood. Malyuta backed from him, holding the baby.

'I am two hundred and thirty-four years old,' said the witch. 'For two hundred of those years I have waited for this child to be born – my child! I am a master of the three magics; I am the harvester of ice-apples. I can heal and I can harm, and I can teach all these things. What can you teach?'

12

Backed against the wall, Malyuta said, 'I shall teach him to hunt.'

'You think that a great thing. Can you teach him to hunt as a bear? Give him to me.'

'I shall teach him to hunt bear!' Malyuta held the baby with one arm and pushed the witch away with the other. 'And until he is big enough for that I shall be a roof to him, a fire for him, a dog to guard him, a wall against the night. I shall never give him to a night-comer, a Ghost-World Walker!'

The witch swung about and returned to the wooden bench. 'When this hour is over, I must go. So let us talk like men at market, Malyuta – yes, I know your name. What can I give you in exchange for your child? What do you want more than him? Do you want to be rich, Malyuta? Do you want enough money to buy your own freedom and your wife's? Then you can sell your furs for your own profit and make yourself rich, and you can get ten sons to replace this one!'

Malyuta felt as if he had been punched, for he knew that the witch could do what he said, and make him a free, rich man. He knew that he could have anything he demanded in exchange for the baby he held – and it was only a baby. Weren't there enough babies in the world? He felt that his arms would move to hand the baby over and, angry with himself for being tempted, he shouted, 'I am no Czar, to buy and sell my children! I have also waited a long time – too long – for this one son, and nothing will buy him from me! If you promised to make me the Czar, I wouldn't give him to you!'

'Is that what you want?' asked Kuzma. 'To be Czar?'

Malyuta's mouth opened and stayed open, and his

13

heart almost stopped as he saw himself as Czar, God on Earth, owning all, ruling all. But he said nothing.

'Would you like to be young again?'

Malyuta held his breath and choked over that offer, and the witch grinned, sure of winning. But Malyuta looked at the midnight sunlight on the rafters, glistening in rainbows on the cobwebs that hung there. He looked at the northern witch sitting on the plain wooden bench, and the ghost-drum lying in a beam of sunlight on the floor. Outside a cow mooed and a bird sang, and about every sight and sound there was the very flavour of a dream. So what did it matter what the witch offered? 'Nothing you can give me will buy my son.'

The witch, too, looked towards the open door, where the midnight sunlight was growing stronger. He rose and came towards Malyuta, his feet padding, his cloak whispering and stinking of bear in the hot room. 'You keep this child because you think he will bring you happiness – but I tell you, not! What you hold there, in your arms, is pain! He is a shaman, a world-walker, a child of the Iron Ash. He was not meant to be a slave's son, fixed in one world. I tell you, little man, keep him and you will lose all that you most value. Black as winter darkness; white as ice; red as blood indeed. Sharp as a sable's bite! He will bring you misery!'

Afraid, Malyuta cried, 'Don't try to curse me!'

'To tell the future is not to curse. Give him to me!'

'No,' said Malyuta, glancing towards the door again, where the light grew brighter and brighter. 'I will never give him to you, not in a dream, and not waking. No matter what you promise, or how you ask, or how you curse. Not for his sake, not for my sake, not for his mother's sake. He is my son, and I shall rear him.'

'Give him to me!' cried the witch, and laid both his strong mittened hands on Malyuta's shoulders, grinning with anger in his face.

'No!'

Now the witch laid his hands on the baby. 'Give him to me, give him!'

'I would sooner give up my own head than this baby!' Malyuta said.

The witch took his hands from the baby and drew back. The sleepers in the room moved in their places, and sighed. The last moments of Midsummer's Day were passing away.

'Two hundred years I've waited for him,' said Kuzma. 'You will have other children; I can have no other. Give him to me.'

'No.'

Midsummer's Day had passed. Then the witch stooped and picked up his ghost-drum from the floor. In his thick, bear-clawed boots he crossed the floor and went out at the door.

Malyuta raised the baby to his shoulder, put his hairy cheek to the baby's soft cheek, and let tears of relief run down his face.

Around him, the sleepers were waking, throwing back their covers and sitting up. Still Malyuta didn't know if he was awake or asleep and dreaming.

'Malyuta's rocking the baby!' people said. 'Have you been standing guard over him all night, Malyuta? Ah, and now he's hungry!' they said, as the baby woke and began to scream in Malyuta's ear.

Malyuta was silent. His head was heavy and dazed. He thought he'd slept and dreamed. A bad dream. A voice, demanding, demanding, stirring the dust between the wooden walls . . . but he couldn't remember what the voice had said. He laid his baby son beside his wife and lay down with them to sleep.

Ambrosi, he thought, as he drifted into sleep. I shall call him Ambrosi, because it means 'Immortal' and so my son is: he's perfect and, to me, he'll live forever.

And that (says the cat) is how Malyuta the Czar's huntsman defied the bear-shaman and denied him his apprentice.

It is never a lucky thing to do (says the cat), to make an enemy of a shaman.

2

The cat walks round and round the tree, its golden chain ringing as acorns fall.

Where did Kuzma go when he left Malyuta (asks the cat)? Listen, and I shall tell you, in a while.

But first I shall tell you of the reindeer, and of the people who follow them.

Far, far from where you are now (says the cat), lost in the blank whiteness of the snow-plain, freezing under the black and silver of the great sky, a reindeer herd is shivering. And close by the herd is a little camp of pointed tents, with sleds outside and dogs lying near them, huddled together to keep warm.

Every year the reindeer herds climb into the mountains to eat the new, sweet spring grass in the mountain meadows. And every year, when the northern winter begins to darken the skies and freeze the ground, the reindeer leave the mountains and return to the lowlands which, though covered deep in snow, are not so cold as the mountains.

And wherever the reindeer go, the people of the tents follow. There would be no life for the people if it were not for the reindeer. Their tents and their sleeping bags and all their clothes are made of reindeer hide, which has this special property: that even when wet, it still keeps the wearer warm.

The milk the people drink is reindeer milk, and their cheese is reindeer-milk cheese. They eat reindeer meat, and they chew lumps of reindeer fat to keep warm. Their tools are made of reindeer antler and reindeer bone, and their wealth is counted by the number of reindeer in the herd they follow. Reindeer pull their sleds, and they even ride on the reindeer's backs.

There would be no life for the people if it were not for the reindeer.

Though it was winter, inside the pointed tents it was warm. In each one, a fire burned and food was cooking, and the small homes were filled with warmth and the smells of meat, of wet dogs, and of wet leather drying. The people sat on the floors of the tents, on reindeer hides and furs, while children and dogs padded about among them. Above their heads, from the poles of the tents, hung all kinds of tools and foods in leather bags, some swinging gently in the rising air from the fire, and making moving shadows on the tents' hide walls.

Against the other side of those thin walls leaned the whole weight of the killing cold and the long winter night; but inside the people talked, and looked at the fire, and pretended that there was no cold.

Inside one tent, there was a quarrel. 'Why won't you lend me your needle?' asked Little Fish.

'I will lend you a needle,' said her sister, White Reindeer, 'but not *that* needle. That is my best needle, and I need it.'

'I need it too,' said Little Fish. 'You know I want to make this coat the best I ever made.'

'Then use this needle – you can have this needle, I give it to you.'

18

'I don't want that one; it's too thick. I've made tiny holes for fine stitching and I need a fine needle. That one would spoil my work.'

'A bad embroideress always blames her tools,' said White Reindeer.

'Oh!' said Little Fish. 'Did you hear that?'

'I thought sisters were supposed to help each other,' said Leaf, who is Little Fish's husband.

White Reindeer said, 'I have offered to give her a needle, to keep. She said she wouldn't take it.'

'Because it's no good!' said Leaf. 'You're hoping that everyone will say you are the best embroideress when you've spoiled Fish's work with your bad needles!'

Beside the fire, sitting cross-legged and patiently carving bone plaques to make his daughter a bangle, sat White Reindeer's husband, Bone Hook. Close beside him lay his youngest son, called Fox for short. He lay with his face close to his father's hands, to watch the carving.

'Oh, why don't you keep your mouth closed, Leaf?' White Reindeer cried. 'Fish and I were good friends before ever you came along – '

'You always bullied her,' said Leaf, and Little Fish nodded.

Fox looked up as his father looked down, and they looked into each other's eyes. They both sighed.

'Bullied her? I, bullied her? She was always spoiled – what a little fat Fish she always was! What happened when I lent her my favourite needle, the best needle I ever had? She broke it, that's what happened – she broke it!'

'Oh, that isn't fair!' Little Fish said. 'It wasn't my fault!'

'Then whose fault was it?' demanded White Reindeer. 'Did it break itself?'

Bone Hook looked down at Fox again, and smiled. Fox smiled back, got up onto his hands and knees and crawled around behind his father until he reached the other three. 'Little Mother!' he said, putting his arms around Little Fish from behind, and hugging her. He kissed the side of her neck, and she was annoyed at being interrupted in her arguing and pushed him away.

'Oh, if you push me away, I'll go to my real mother,' he said, and crawled on to White Reindeer, who he also hugged and kissed. She didn't push him away, but asked,

'What do you want?'

'I want my mothers to stop quarrelling,' he said. 'I want my other father to stop quarrelling. It's giving me an ache in the ear.'

'You want your mother to keep her needle,' Leaf said.

'I'll give Leaf a hug, he's so bad-tempered,' Fox said, and began crawling over the hides to him.

'No, get off, get off!' Leaf said, but began to laugh, even though he didn't want to, as Fox threw himself on him in a ferocious hug. 'Do you think you're a bear, you skinny little thing?' And Leaf broke free of Fox, threw him on his back and held him down while he kicked.

'Oh, now don't start fighting, don't start,' Little Fish said. 'I don't want to be hit.' She hitched herself away from them, pulling the tunic she was working on with her.

Leaf let Fox up, and Fox crawled back to White Reindeer. 'Let my other mother borrow the needle,' he said. 'I know she won't break it.'

'Oh, and how do you know?' White Reindeer asked.

'I know she'll be so, so careful with it,' Fox said, looking at Little Fish.

'Of course I will,' said Little Fish. 'I'm always careful. I didn't mean to break the other one – it was an accident.'

'It was an accident, Mother,' said Fox, kissing her. 'And Father will make you a new one, better than that one, in case it gets broken.'

'And I'll give you some of my silver thread,' said Little Fish.

'Oh, there's no need for that,' said White Reindeer. 'Now you make me feel spiteful . . .' She was opening the soft leather roll in which she kept her needles. 'But if it's broken – ' she said, wagging her finger at her son, Fox.

'If it's broken, you can have my head,' he said.

She laughed and leaned her own head close to his. 'I'd rather have your tongue.'

'If the needle's broken, you can have my tongue for a shoe-sole,' Fox said.

'Better have it for a honeycomb,' Little Fish said, all smiles as her sister passed her the needle.

'Come here, Fox, spit in my tea and sweeten it,' said Leaf.

'The fox bit him, true enough,' said White Reindeer proudly.

All this time Bone Hook had sat silently by the fire, chipping away bone from his carving, but listening. He smiled, with a pride equal to his wife's, and nodded to himself.

In the stories the reindeer people tell there are foxes, and the little foxes are always quick-witted, and they always have clever, sweet, soft words to gentle the anger of the bear, to outwit the lynx, to charm the fish from the

21

stream. Long ago the people decided that Bone Hook's youngest son must have been bitten by a fox, and the fox's bite infected him with the same sweetness of words. He is known as Fox for short. Bitten-by-a-Fox is his full name.

Now the quarrel was over, Bitten-by-a-Fox crawled back over the hides to his place beside his father. Bone Hook looked down at him, and smiled a wrinkled, slit-eyed smile, and then went on carving.

Bone Hook is the leader the people don't know they have. They are all family, these people, brothers and sisters, mothers and fathers, uncles and aunts, by marriage if not by blood. If they were asked: Who is your leader? they would answer: We don't have one, we don't need one. No one makes rules for us.

But, whenever the reindeer people met strangers, they would all look at Bone Hook, and then they would all shuffle backwards until Bone Hook was left alone to do the talking for all of them.

Whenever any of the people fell out, and their quarrel was disturbing everyone, and there seemed no end to it, soon everyone would begin to say: What do you think, Bone Hook? Don't you agree with us? You can't agree with them! And then everyone would wait happily for Bone Hook to point out the rights and wrongs on both sides, and find a solution.

And whenever there was a bigger decision to be made, such as who should go hunting and who should stay at home, or whether a certain marriage proposal should be accepted, then it was to Bone Hook that everyone came for advice.

But still Bone Hook worked, like everyone else, and lived in a tent no better than the other tents. When food was short, he went hungry, like everyone else, and if he were ever to call himself their leader, the people would have been angry.

But Bone Hook knew that he was the leader, and it pleased him to see his youngest son so quick to settle quarrels. The reindeer people's life was hard: they must always be ready to help each other, to feed and clothe, protect and defend each other. Quarrels were something they could not afford.

And I, thought Bone Hook, am growing old. Years of squinting into the sun against the glare of the snow had made his face brown, had creased it into hundreds of fine lines, and had turned his eyes to slits. These days, when he rose in the morning, he was stiff and limped and hobbled about his work for hours before he could move easily. He knew that he could not live for many more years, and he was afraid that, when he died, his people would not hold together, but would allow their quarrels and disagreements to split them; and that made him sad. But now he had hopes that his son, his youngest, his little Fox, would slip into his place as the leader that the people didn't know they had, and the people wouldn't even notice that Bone Hook had gone! This thought made Bone Hook happy. And he thought that, if he could make the people turn to Bitten-by-a-Fox with their problems even before his own death, then that would be best.

So, whenever Bone Hook was asked to find the answer to some problem, he would call to Fox, and ask his advice before everyone. And even when Fox made a silly answer – he was still young – Bone Hook was careful to let everyone see that he listened and took the answer seriously. And often, Fox made good answers.

23

Soon, thought Bone Hook, it would come as naturally to the people to ask Bitten-by-a-Fox for advice as to ask Bone Hook.

Bitten-by-a-Fox watched his father carving until his eyes grew tired. The gentle chatting of the other people in the tent and the warmth of the fire made him settle himself comfortably on the reindeer hides, and place his hands under his head. With his eyes closed, all sounds became more clear to him. He heard the bone chipping under his father's knife, and the sizzling and hissing of the fire. Voices crooned, and feet shifted on the hides and, from above, came the sound of the wind sighing around the tent poles and moaning over the open smoke-hole. He listened more and more to the sound of the wind, and the outside sounds. The shifting of the reindeer came through the ground to his ear, and dogs grumbled and yelped. But as Fox sank deeper towards sleep, the earth under his ear rumbled. The reindeer were wheeling and stamping and the dogs began to howl – cold sounds from the outside cold.

Bitten-by-a-Fox sat up. He saw that everyone had stopped talking and working. Everyone was listening to the sounds from the darkness.

Bone Hook dropped the bone and knife, pulled on his tall red hat and thick mittens, and crawled towards the tent flap. Leaf came crawling too, bringing his spear with him, and Bitten-by-a-Fox was quick to pull his cap down over his head and ears, pull on his coat and mittens, and crawl out of the tent after his father and uncle.

Other fathers, sons and brothers were crawling out from the other tents, out into the shock of cold and darkness and the wind that scratched their faces and soughed in their ears.

Trampling the snow, they came together, asking each other what had frightened the dogs and the reindeer, and looking about them to see what it could have been. And then they saw. It was a white bear.

Of all the bears, the white bear is the biggest and the fiercest. It fears nothing and can run over the snow faster than a reindeer, faster than a dog-team can pull a sled. It walks upright like a man when it pleases, and it can understand human speech, so it must never be named, or it will hear and come, to see why it is being called. The white bear is so wise that when the north freezes and the long night of half a year sets in, the bear dies a little death and lies asleep until spring, when it comes to life again.

Through a mist of darkness half melted by snow-light, a white bear came treading softly towards the reindeer people's camp. Its head snaked forward on its long neck, its shoulders humped, and all the weight of the black sky and sharp stars pressed down on its back.

The reindeer scattered widely as the bear came through them, and the men looked at each other in amazement and fright. The bear should not have been there – bears keep to the sea-coast where they hunt seals. It should not have been there – bears sleep through the winter. But there the bear was, and who dares to tell the white bear where and when he can walk?

'Who spoke his name?' Leaf shouted; but no one answered that.

The men pointed their spears at the bear, but none of them had the nerve to attack. They sent quick glances from the bear to Bone Hook, and waited for Bone Hook to tell them what to do. Even Bitten-by-a-Fox waited for his father to speak, but Bone Hook only held his spear ready, like the rest, and waited.

The bear stopped in front of them and swung its head to and fro on the end of its long neck, as if it was trying to catch a whiff of the women and children in the tents. Bitten-by-a-Fox looked again at his father, and wondered why Bone Hook said nothing. Then Bitten-by-a-Fox couldn't wait any longer and spoke to the bear himself.

'We wish good wishes for you, Grandfather,' he said. 'Why have you come to visit us?'

The bear lifted up its big, clawed front feet and slowly raised itself until it stood on its hind legs. It was seven feet tall, overtopping every man there.

Then the bear raised its front paws to its nose and seemed to push back its own head. The fur of its belly parted and fell aside, like the two sides of a cloak. The long-snouted head fell backwards, and there stood a tall, thickset man whose narrow, wrinkled face peered from a mass of grey and black hair. He wore a cloak made from a white bear's skin, and the bear's head dangled on his shoulders.

People who had been peering from the tents ducked back inside; and among those outside ran a whisper: 'Shaman!' Only a shaman could change his shape and appear as a bear. But the man had no other sign of the shaman about him, no staff and no ghost-drum. Still, it would be best to treat him with caution and good manners. Fearing to take their eyes from the visitor for too long, the men flicked glances between him and Bone Hook. But still Bone Hook said nothing.

It was again Bitten-by-a-Fox who spoke. 'You're

welcome, Grandfather,' he said. 'Come into my father's tent, warm yourself, and eat with us.'

The man in the bearskin smiled, wrinkling his face even more and showing large, strong teeth. He nodded his head in thanks, and walked through the line of men – who backed away. The shaman ducked into the light and warmth of Bone Hook's tent as Bitten-by-a-Fox held up the tent flap for him.

Outside, the other men called their families from the other tents, and people began bundling themselves into warm clothes, calling out to each other and scrambling from the tents into the darkness, before squeezing, a moment later, into the light and warmth of the tent that held the visitor.

The tent was soon crowded. Children were dragged onto laps to make more room, and people hugged their knees to their chests, or pressed themselves against their neighbours' backs. The heat of so many people, added to that of the fire, soon became stiflingly warm, and tunics were pulled off over heads. Food was passed round, clumsily, because hands were always bumping elbows and heads. The visitor, sitting on his white bearskin, was given strips of dried reindeer meat and preserved cloudberries. He ate, and grinned at the curious faces all around him, at the eyes that stared and then quickly looked away if he looked at them. They were afraid of him, and afraid of the bear he had been; and the visitor enjoyed their fear.

For a long while no one – not even Bitten-by-a-Fox – dared to speak to the shaman, though they offered him whatever they happened to have in their hand at that moment – reindeer cheese, a cup of thick, buttered tea, a chunk of reindeer fat. They were afraid of angering him. It is never wise to anger a shaman.

But the frightened silence went on so long that it began to seem insulting to their guest. Smiles and polite offers of food were not enough to make a guest feel welcome. The reindeer people began to look hard at Bone Hook, willing him to find something to say. Others began to stare at, even to nudge, Bitten-by-a-Fox. But it was the shaman himself who broke the silence. 'Shall I pay for my lodging with a story? I know them all.'

The people straightened where they sat, hugged children gleefully and smiled, and whispered together. They loved to hear stories. New story-tellers were always welcome; and this story-teller was a shaman, who would tell his story with all the mastery of word-magic. Yes, they nodded to Bone Hook; say yes. But Bone Hook smiled and left the answering to his youngest son.

'Tell us the story you tell best, please, Grandfather,' Bitten-by-a-Fox said.

The shaman smiled.

'I'll tell a tale you know well,' he began, and there was a shuffling and a sighing as the crowded people pressed still closer and settled to hear. 'I tell of brothers, of Balder and Loki.'

A murmur rose suddenly from the people, and as instantly died. They knew the story. It was a good story.

Balder, said the shaman, *was the best of young men: so beautiful that to look at him gave others pleasure; so kind and generous that all had cause to love him; so honest and loyal that no one feared any slight from him; and he was strong and warm-fleshed also. Where he came, summer followed; and while Balder lived, summers were long, light and hot, full of* birth and growth. While Balder lived, in those first times, Summer was All. There was no winter, no cold, no dark, and no death. No one, in those first times, knew the road that leads to the Ghost World. The gate to the Ghost World was closed, and it had never opened. How many, many of us wish it had never opened!

But beautiful Balder, young and warm, had a brother who was not beautiful or strong, and his name was Loki. It seemed to Loki that all warmth and love streamed away from him to Balder, making Balder still more beautiful, while he, Loki – Loki was left to stand alone in darkness and cold, growing ever more ugly. It was not easy for Loki to be generous or kind. He was the less loved because of it, and the shadows and the chill gathered about him. Loki was the first to know darkness and cold. So, 'As cold as Loki's heart,' we say, and we call winter, 'Loki's breath.'

But Loki was clever. He looked into his darkness and he learned from what he saw there – Loki was the first shaman. When Balder slept, Loki entered his dreams by paths he had learned in darkness; and into Balder's dreams he brought shadows. Balder dreamt of injury and death; of his own injury, his own death – things that had never been known in those first times. Balder, beautiful Balder, was the first to have bad dreams! Again and again Balder woke in terror until he was afraid to sleep – and, as he tired, so his beauty and warmth were dimmed, and Loki – Loki was glad.

But the other people of those times loved Balder and were afraid for him. When he told them of his dreams, they said to each other, 'What can we do to keep these dreams from him?' And Frigga, the mother of Balder and Loki, said, 'I shall travel across the world, and ask every thing under our sky to promise not to harm him.'

Frigga began her long journey, in her cart drawn by wolves:

*a long, long journey, my friends, and a long, long asking —
quick for me to tell, but long to do! To every thing under the sky
Frigga spoke: every animal, every fish, every bird, every thing
that crawls on the earth: every plant, every bush, every tree:
every stone, every boulder, every mountain, every hill: every
river, every stream, every pool, every spring, every lake: for
they all have spirits within them which may hate or love.*

*Balder was loved, and the promises were given freely, gladly,
from every thing under the sky: they would do no harm to
Balder.*

*It was Loki the promises harmed. Every proof of the love the
world had for his brother hurt him the more. If you would know
how much, lift the tent-flap! Look into the dark and the cold out
there and you will know the feelings of Loki when he measured
the love the world had for his brother against the love it had for
him.*

*When Frigga returned to the people, bringing with her the
world's promises, she was as welcome as her news. And Frigga
herself tested the worth of the promises by picking up a clod of
earth and throwing it at Balder. The clod turned aside before it
reached him, because Earth had promised never to hurt him.
Then the people began a new game. They threw stones, and
knives, and logs and axes at Balder, as if they meant to kill him
— but everything they threw turned aside before it reached him,
and fell harmlessly to the ground. Balder stood still and let
them throw, because he trusted in the love of the world.
Nothing hurt him.*

*Loki didn't join the game, but stood watching and feeling the
cold of winter in his heart, in his bones' marrow. Then he went
away, found Frigga and said to her, 'What a great thing you've
done! How patient, how brave you are! Have you honestly
spoken with every thing under the sky?'*

Frigga, poor Frigga, never suspected why Loki questioned

her, and she answered him willingly: 'Yes, every thing under the sky!'

'Every thing?' asked Loki. 'Even the lichens on the rocks, even the moss, even the tiny flies that fill the air in summer?'

'Even they,' said Frigga, 'and more than they.' But then she paused, and smiled. 'There was one thing . . .' she said. 'It was so weak – it had no strength of its own, but had to cling and feed on an oak. What harm could such a thing do Balder? So I have no promise from the mistletoe.'

As soon as he found this out, Loki left Frigga, and went to find the mistletoe. He sang to it, and told it that he was killing it because he needed its help; and then he cut it and shaped it into a dart, which he carried to where the people were shooting arrows and throwing spears at Balder.

Among them came Loki, with his ally the mistletoe, which had not been given the chance to say that it loved Balder and would spare him. Loki threw the dart, and it buried itself in Balder's heart and killed him. No one knew who had thrown the dart. It might have been any of those gathered there.

The shaman suddenly laughed, and the harsh sound of his laughter broke the spell his gentle voice had laid on his listeners, so that they started and stared about them at the firelight and shadows, bewildered. The shaman laughed louder when he saw their shocked faces, wrinkling up his sharp-nosed face and baring his long teeth. The people looked at each other, and smiled to please the shaman, but they saw nothing to laugh at in the story, and their smiles quickly faded. Then the shaman took up his tale again, and as soon as he did, the people drew deep breaths and resettled, with mouths slack and eyes fixed on the visions his words made in the rising smoke of the fire.

So Balder died, said the shaman, smiling, *died, and was*

31

the first to walk the road to the Ghost World, the first for whom the Ghost World Gate swung open. It closed behind him, and would not open for him again because of the mistletoe dart held deep in his heart. And his people, left behind . . . They had no practice in death . . . This was the first death! Theirs was the first grieving and the harshest; the first sorrow ever known in this world and the greatest! Hark! cried the shaman, and raised a finger as the wind howled softly round the tent, died to a moan and soughed again. *The cold, the dark, the ice, the thin-edged wind: that is the sorrow of Balder's people for his loss: and Loki's sorrow. Balder could never return to them: and so winter followed winter without break. There was no sun for the people bereft of Balder, no light, no warmth. Summer died with Balder, and there was eternal winter. 'This grief is too great,' said Frigga. 'It cannot be borne. Balder must return, though I break the boundaries between worlds. The gate must open again.' And so said every thing under the freezing sky.*

'Who can make this journey?' Frigga asked. 'Who will go through the Ghost World Gate?'

'I will go,' said Loki, first of shamans; and so Loki was the first of the living to walk the road to the Ghost World, following the path he had learned in his darkness. He passed through the Ghost World Gate, and found his way through Iron Wood, and came to that palace built of Loss and Sorrow, where lives Hel, the Ghost World's Queen. Her palace is guarded by fierce wolves and bears, whose fur is matted with blood, but Loki spoke gently to them, and passed them by and entered the palace. It was empty and silent then, as it is full and silent now . . . The dead cannot speak unless the visitor to their world speaks first. Through hall after silent hall went Loki until he came to the place of honour, where sat Balder, still beautiful, but staring at his brother with a sadness that his living face had

32

never shown. But Balder could say nothing: the first of the dead could speak no more than can the last.

Beside Balder sat Hel. Half of her is a beautiful woman, but half of her is a corpse, discoloured and perfumed with decay. To Loki, she said, 'I know you are a living man – your steps shake the walls of my hall. How do you dare come here?'

'Lady,' said Loki, 'I am a messenger'; and he gave her Frigga's message, and told her of the sorrow that was in the world for Balder's loss. 'We beg you, Lady, open the Ghost World Gate, let him return to us.'

Said Hel, 'Have I waited so long to greet my first guest to turn him from my door so soon? And shall I send Balder from here, where there is no other beauty? No. I shall not let him go.'

'Lady,' said Loki, 'my brother's light shines dimly here, in your dark halls; his warmth is feeble against your cold – but when he lived, he lit and warmed the Earth. And the whole Earth grieves for his loss, and longs for his return. I beg you, let him come back to us.'

'I have heard the people grieving for him,' said Hel. 'It is fine music. But does the whole world grieve for him? I think not. Let me hear the weeping and lamenting of every thing under your sky. I would think the release of Balder a small price to pay for such music.'

'Lady,' said Loki, 'every thing under the sky shall weep.' And with one parting look to his beautiful, silent brother, Loki left that place and returned through the Gate to our world.

He brought his message to the people: every thing under the sky must weep for Balder if they wished his return. 'Then Balder is ours again!' cried Frigga. 'Nothing under the sky will refuse to weep.'

Riders were sent over the whole world, crying as they rode, 'Weep, weep for Balder! If you would have him return, then let

*your tears be the river on which he sails from Hel's lands!'
Wherever the messengers passed, men sat down and wept for
lost Balder. Women bowed their heads into their hands and
wept for him, or raised their heads and lamented to the sky.
Children lay down and wept into the earth. Every animal,
every tree, every plant, every stone – all things under the sky
wept for Balder, lost. Look!*

As he spoke, the shaman lifted up a knife that had
been brought into the warm tent from the cold outside.
Its blade was covered with droplets of water that ran
from it when he tilted it.

*See: the knife still weeps for Balder's loss, even now. Then
the whole world, the whole sky, rang with mourning. But, on a
cold mountain side a messenger came upon a giantess, an ugly,
unloved creature, who scowled and shook her head, and
laughed but would not weep. 'Did Balder care for me?' she
asked. 'Would I be so ugly if his light had ever shone on me?
Would I be so alone if his warmth had ever touched me? Let Hel
keep what she has. I shall never weep but for myself.'*

*And Hel said, 'I love the sound of grief, but I missed the
giantess' tears. All things under the sky wept for Balder, but
not she, not she, and her dry eyes are the locks, her laughter the
chains that keep Balder my prisoner for ever. But come, you
who love Balder. The road is known now, the Gate will open –
come to my halls, to my Iron Wood, come to Balder. Come
home.'*

*And, in the darkness of every winter, friends, then and now,
many, many of us, young and old, follow Balder home. Winter
and Death have never left us, nor ever will. Balder has never
returned to us, and never will.*

But who was the giantess who would not weep? asked the
shaman, smiling. *To answer that you must ask yourselves:
Who was it took darkness into Balder's dreams? Who wheedled*

from Frigga the secret of the mistletoe? Who was it went to the Ghost World and learned, before any other, the bargain Hel made?

And yet, I know it is true that Loki loved Balder and the world – indeed, loved them more than any other, for he knew their darkness as well as their light, their cold as well as their warmth, their silence as well as their speech, and he loved them still. And many times has Loki, the shaman, journeyed to that fearful palace beyond the Ghost World's Gate and Iron Wood, to kiss his brother Balder, and bring us back a short summer.

The shaman closed his mouth on those words, and there was no more story.

The people sat as if still listening, with open mouths and eyes glazed to see nothing but the pictures the words made. Tears ran down many of the faces into the open mouths, and from all about the tent came sobs and snuffles and gulps as, yet again, they wept for Balder without saving him. They drew deep breaths, and could hardly realize that the story had ended. When, one by one, they did, and looked about them, the firelight was dimmed and the tent was darker. A sweet, painful sadness rose from them with their sighs, and was breathed in again and again, until it ached under their hearts. A sadness for Balder, and winter, and death, and that stories must end.

But then they blinked, wiped their faces and laughed at their own tears. Many hands stretched out at once to offer food to their story-teller: flat cakes of rye-bread, bilberries and smoked fish were poked at him from all sides.

'That was a fine telling, Grandfather,' said Bitten-by-a-Fox, his voice shaking a little. 'The best we ever heard.'

The shaman smiled and accepted a rye-cake from him.

Leaf thought they should know more about their guest, but to ask a direct question would be rude. So he said, 'You must have had a long, cold journey to come here, Grandfather.'

'A bear travels fast and warm,' said the story-teller, and grinned at the shock that showed in the faces and sudden, fidgeting movements of all the people in the tent. They had not expected him to speak so openly of his shape-shifting.

Bone Hook glared at Leaf, but the shaman looked around at them all with slow amusement. The firelight shone brightly in his dark eyes and on the wetness of the white teeth that grinned through his beard. 'If you want to know who I am,' he said to Leaf, 'my name is Kuzma.' Only a powerful shaman, one so powerful that he had no need to fear anyone would dare to tell his name to strangers. And now the visitor was looking Bone Hook in the eyes, waiting for Bone Hook to tell his name, as was only polite when the guest had told his.

Bone Hook chose to be rude, rather than tell. He coughed, looked away from Kuzma, and said nothing. Others have power over you when they know your name. They call your name, and you are made to look up. And a shaman can use your name for greater magics than that. To excuse his rudeness, Bone Hook took some dried fish from his wife's lap and offered it to Kuzma.

Kuzma didn't accept the fish, but looked around him again. The people sitting nearest the shaman shuffled away from him as far as the crowded tent would allow them, fearing that he had taken offence at Bone Hook's refusal to tell his name. Kuzma's long nose wrinkled and his eyes narrowed to slits as he studied them: his strong teeth shone from his shaggy growth of grey and black hair. And yet there was something sad about the very fierceness of his smile.

'Why do you fear me?' he said. 'I came in bear shape because, sometimes, I wish not to be a man; but when I scented you, and heard your voices, then I longed for company. And have I harmed you?'

They said nothing; but their bodies hunched away from him.

'I did not choose to walk the Ghost World paths,' Kuzma said. 'I am a child of the Iron Ash. On the night of my birth, a shaman claimed me as his apprentice. He took me to the far north, where the ice-apples grow, away from all people, away from the world.'

The vast loneliness of the snow-plains, and the dark sky seemed to creep into the tent at the shaman's slow words.

'He sang me out of my childhood,' said Kuzma, 'and he taught me the three great magics; he gave me three hundred years of life and, his own life ended, he went into the Ghost World, to sleep in the Ash until it was time for him to be reborn. And I – I have lived my whole life alone, waiting for the spirits to tell me that my own apprentice was born. Waiting and waiting, and gathering the ice-apples until I think I am as cold as they. Two hundred years I have waited, and my apprentice is born at last . . . And I am denied him.'

Children were hugged tight and passed from lap to lap, so they should be far from the shaman. Kuzma saw how the children were protected from him, and he smiled again, a sad, fierce smile. 'A shaman must have an apprentice,' he said, 'to keep alive what his long life has taught him. What good to live three hundred years if everything of that three hundred years goes into the

Ghost World and is forgotten? And if I cannot have the apprentice born for me, then I must look for one elsewhere . . . Isn't that so?' Kuzma asked, and smiled into Bone Hook's face.

'You have the world to search, Grandfather,' Bone Hook said, while all his people sat stiff and afraid, making not even the softest sound.

'If my child is refused me, then all the world and everything in it is alike to me,' Kuzma said. 'Why should I not take one of these little ones? You have enough and to spare.'

Bone Hook stared back into Kuzma's black eyes and said nothing. The crowded tent was filled with sudden, spasmic movement as mothers and fathers gripped their children and made to rise, to escape. Then they sank back among their friends, holding their children, holding their breaths; thinking, like hunted animals, that their best safety lay in keeping utterly still.

'You are joking with us, Grandfather,' Bone Hook said gently.

'You hope that I am,' Kuzma said, 'but I am not. No. I shall choose a child and carry it away. I shall sing it from its childhood: I shall sing it away from those who loved it. I shall take it by the hand and lead it into the Ghost World, and then it can never be happy among your kind . . . But it will be a shaman! It will live three hundred years! Which child shall I take?'

Kuzma began to look about the tent. He held out his hand to a toddler, who pressed against its father and hid its face. He leaned to a terrified woman and drew the coverings from the face of her baby, peering at it, sharp-nosed. The people were looking in desperation at Bone Hook, who sat with a tightly closed mouth.

Bitten-by-a-Fox had been watching his father, waiting for him to outwit the shaman with words, as surely his father could. But Bone Hook said nothing, and his face frightened Bitten-by-a-Fox. His father's face was afraid, as if there was nothing he could say.

So Bitten-by-a-Fox looked into the shaman's face and said, 'Grandfather, you are too good to rob us of a child when we have taken you in and fed you – you are too great a man to be so unkind; you would not do that to us, Grandfather.'

Kuzma's grin only became more wicked, and his eyes more sad. 'You are the one they call Fox-Bitten, are you not?' he said. 'Such sweet words, such soft words. Do you think a shaman can be caught in such simple word-nets, boy? You fed me, you sheltered me, yes, but not from love. From fear.'

'Then have pity on our fear, Grandfather,' Fox said. 'Don't take a child from us; don't make us grieve as the world grieved for Balder. Leave us our children, and you will always be welcome in our tents and to all we have.'

'I am feared everywhere, and so welcome every-where,' Kuzma said. 'Even if I ate your children, one by one, I would still be welcome here in your tents, because you would not dare to turn me away. And I want only one child, Fox, just one little child from your many, Foxy, just one baby, to be my apprentice. I will leave you the rest.'

The shaman laughed to himself, for he knew how much he asked. Fox and Bone Hook looked at each other in despair, while the rest of the people looked at them. Whichever family lost its child would blame all the others, who had kept their children. The loss of that one child would cause bitterness and quarrels far into the future. At every slight, the family who had lost their child would remember their loss, and would bring it up again, and would be less willing to help the other families. And when life is hard, as it was for the reindeer people, everyone must willingly help each other.

At last Bone Hook spoke. He reached out and put a hand on Fox's shoulder, and then said to the shaman: 'We will never give you a child, though you may take one.'

Kuzma laughed again, and began to look slowly around the tent. It was clear that not one child was hidden from him, though they had been pushed behind their parents' backs, and wrapped in robes.

Bitten-by-a-Fox couldn't bear the shaman's gloating. There are times, he thought, when sweet words are not enough: times when even the clever fox must bite. 'You will take no child from this tent!' he said.

Even in the midst of their dread for their children, the people were surprised to hear such harsh words from him and looked round. Kuzma looked at him too, and laughed at him.

Then Fox drew his knife from his belt and pointed it at the shaman. To threaten a guest is the worst of manners. 'No child from this tent!'

Bone Hook fastened his hand about his son's wrist and forced the knife down. But Kuzma had risen to his feet. Before any apology could be made, Kuzma began to chant.

My words shall be, he said, *my words shall be. The sea wave rises to the shore, and falls back. The sun rises, the sun sinks.*

As light turns to dark, so dark turns to light. Only change is everlasting, and I curse you with change, everlasting change. My words shall be.

In darkness, you shall be wolves. Change! Your eyes shall become wolves' eyes. See as wolves see! Your ears shall become wolves' ears. Hear as wolves hear! Your mouths shall become wolves' mouths. Eat as wolves eat! Your throats shall become wolves' throats. Cry as wolves cry! Your hands, your feet shall become wolves' feet. Run as wolves run! Your every part shall become a wolf's part and you shall be wolves wholly. Change! My words shall be!

Still standing among the people as they scrambled to leave the tent, Kuzma howled like a wolf. The people's legs changed into wolves' legs beneath them and tripped them. The human clothes they wore hindered their new bodies. They tried to cry out to Kuzma, to beg him to stop, but heard themselves growling and whimpering like wolves. They looked around and, instead of their friends, they saw the glaring and terrified eyes of wolves. Music and words are the most powerful magics. When a shaman twines them together, all who hear must obey. Change into wolves! said the shaman's song; and the people changed.

Only change is everlasting, Kuzma chanted. *The seed changes to the shoot, the shoot changes to the plant, the flower changes to the fruit, the fruit changes to the seed. I curse you with everlasting change. Be wolves by darkness; change with the light. Be wolves by darkness; change with the light. The summer is short; the winter long. With the dark comes your wolf-shape. My words shall be! My words shall rise with the sun and speak in the darkness. My words shall flower with the spring and fall with the snow. My words shall be! Wolves by*

41

darkness; people by light. Change Everlasting! I curse you with
everlasting change!

Then Kuzma, angry and laughing, tore down the tent
around himself, forcing apart the poles and throwing
aside the reindeer hides. The wolves fled from him,
struggling under the hides, racing away in silent terror.
Not a sound came from them: all their strength was for
running.

Kuzma stood under the black sky full of stars, and
watched the wolves run and vanish into the melting
darkness of snow-light.

Then Kuzma wrapped his bearskin round him, pulling the head of the bear over his own. He dropped
forward, as if to his hands and knees, and a white,
snake-necked, hump-shouldered bear walked away
from where he had stood until the bear too vanished in
the mist of snow-light and darkness.

Between the white snow and the black sky, the
reindeer wandered, with no one to follow them. Confused and lonely dogs wandered about the wreckage of
the tent and the abandoned sled, and yapped at the
wolves who ran about the camp. And snow fell.

And where did Kuzma go this time (asks the cat)?
Kuzma went into the Ghost World. He cut his spell into
a reindeer's shoulder blade, and he climbed the Iron Ash
that grows at the wood's centre. Right to the top of that
tree he climbed, passing many nests, until he found one
where a black sable slept. Into that nest he tossed the
bark and the spell. 'When my apprentice is a shaman,'
he said, 'when he knows the paths to the Ghost World,
he may break this spell. I never shall.'

A fierce spell, then: a spell that would hold in two

worlds; and would never end until light stopped following dark, or summer stopped following winter: or until Ambrosi travelled to the Ghost World and climbed the Iron Ash.

3

Round and round the oak the cat walks, winding up her golden chain.

What (asks the cat) became of the wolves who had been people? What became of Kuzma? That (says the cat) I shall tell later.

For now, do you remember Malyuta, the hunter who refused Kuzma his apprentice? Do you remember Malyuta's baby son, whom he named Immortal – Ambrosi?

Now (says the cat) I tell of Ambrosi and his growing.

Before Ambrosi was one year old, his mother died, having never been well since his birth. He missed her for a little while, but there were many people in the house to pick him up and hug him, talk to him and play with him. When the Ghost World Gate closes behind people like Yefrosinia, it closes for ever; but Ambrosi was too young to understand what 'for ever' means.

But his granny and grandfather had lost their eldest daughter, and they knew all too well the meaning of 'for ever'. And Malyuta, who had waited so long for a wife, and whose heart had opened and closed around the wife he had taken at last; what did he feel?

It often happened that an animal, caught by the foot in one of Malyuta's traps, would be in such pain, and filled with such fear and desperation, that it would chew through its own flesh and bite off its own foot. Malyuta was held in grief, in the trap of Yefrosinia's death. If chewing off his hand would have freed him from it, he would have done that. But he could not free himself from the trap. He could only wait for it to rust away.

Malyuta looked at his little son, and saw all that was left of Yefrosinia on Earth. She had been dark-haired, though her little son was darker. Malyuta would comb his fingers through Ambrosi's thick, heavy, wiry hair, and would feel the touch of his wife's hair on his skin. In time Yefrosinia's face, in his memory, blended with Ambrosi's living face, and he forgot that Yefrosinia had not really been pretty. He began to say that Ambrosi was the image of his mother. He wanted to believe that it was so because, if it was not, then he had no memory of Yefrosinia at all.

Ambrosi was a strong child, quick to run, to discover and ask. He was beautiful too, burning with the brightness of contrast. His dark eyes and hair were startling against his pale skin; and his warm blood glowed through his cheeks and lips. Visitors to the house would watch him and tell his granny, or Malyuta, how pretty he was. Malyuta would proudly remember how miraculous Ambrosi's birth had seemed to him; and this vivid child, this living fragment of his dead wife, still seemed miraculous. He would catch Ambrosi as he ran past, lift him up and kiss him, hug him close and say, 'More treasure I have here than lies in all the Czar's store-houses!'

'Aye,' the visitor would say. 'Our only treasure is our children.' And Malyuta would be secretly offended at the thought that his fellow-slave was comparing his own blob-faced, colourless, snotty-nosed brats to his wonderful Ambrosi.

But to love deeply is to invite Misery to live with you. Malyuta had loved Yefrosinia, and she had died. Loving Ambrosi didn't ease that pain, but only gave him more. When he picked Ambrosi up and hugged the child's small, soft, solid body to him he felt, with agony, the frailty of that body, and feared the many, many things that could break into it and harm it. Seeing the child run, he adored the beauty and strength of the sight, but feared that Ambrosi would fall. Seeing Ambrosi happy, Malyuta felt again, and with added sharpness, the pains that must come to every happy, trusting child: the pain of loss, of betrayal, of disappointment. Yet how can a child be kept from such pain, except by shutting him away in a box, and so causing pain of another kind?

It was pain to Malyuta that, every winter, he had to leave the village and leave his child behind. It was little comfort that he left Ambrosi in the care of a granny and grandad, of aunts and uncles, who all loved him. None of them love him as I do, Malyuta thought; to none of them is he the miracle he is to me. They have other grandchildren, and children of their own, and they only have to be careless of him for a few minutes . . . A few minutes was long enough for a child to fall through ice and drown; long enough for a child to set itself alight at the stove; long enough for a child to wander away and become lost in the cold darkness. And even the most loving and watchful relatives can do nothing if some murderous disease lays hold of a child.

What if Malyuta, returning after his long winter absence, found nothing but Ambrosi's grave waiting for him? What if he must live with Ambrosi's memory fading in his mind, as his wife's memory was fading, until he could no longer remember the looks of either? This was the dread, heavy and sore, that he carried away with him into the winter darkness.

Why do I go? he asked himself. Why do I go, alone, into winter? Why not stay behind, with all the rest; close the door against the dark and open the stove door to see the firelight?

He had to go, because he belonged to the Czar, and the Czar wanted furs.

But still, as Malyuta made his way further and further from the village, it seemed that the village was his heart and that with every step away he was dragging his heart out of his body. And he mourned to himself: Why do I go? Why do I go?

In spring, with what speed, with what lightness and relief Malyuta returned, bringing with him food and presents. And he found that his little boy, his Czar's treasure, his Ambrosi, didn't remember who he was, and hid from him behind his granny's skirts. That, too, was pain for Malyuta.

'This is your daddy, this is Malyuta,' said the granny. 'I've told you about him; you remember. Kiss your daddy, Ambrusha.'

But little Ambrosi didn't like big Malyuta's hairy face, or his stink of sweat and blood, or his loud, harsh voice, and wouldn't go to him. Hunters know how to be patient, though. Malyuta lay in wait for Ambrosi, keeping quiet and still, and watching. He held out his bait of toys and dried or sugared fruit, and soon Ambrosi was setting his foot on the bench between Malyuta's legs, and so mounting, unasked but always welcome, into his father's lap and arms.

Then Malyuta would get down on all fours and let Ambrosi ride on his back, or he would chase the child among the wooden stools and benches, growling, until Ambrosi's wild laughter quavered into tears at the hugeness and ferocity of this great, bearded bear. But once granny had soothed him, he would swagger out from behind her and run laughing at the bear, his father, to start the game again.

He liked to hear Malyuta's stories about animals, especially the stories about bears. 'A bear comes into this house at night,' he told Malyuta.

Malyuta widened his eyes. 'A bear? Into this house?'

'Yes. It comes and looks at me when I'm lying in my bed.'

Which was why Ambrosi was glad to sleep with his father instead of his granny, because he could see that his father was bigger and stronger than his granny, and could easily chase the bear away if it became fierce.

'The bear told me – ' Ambrosi began, but broke off because his attention was taken by a broken scarlet thread in the embroidery of Malyuta's shirt.

'The bear told you?' Malyuta prompted.

'The bear told me . . . there is a tall tree, the bear said. In an iron wood and – ' He drew a deep breath while pulling as hard as he could at the scarlet thread. 'And there are nests in the branches – '

'There are nests in all trees,' Malyuta said, but when Ambrosi was asleep he told the granny that Ambrosi was having nightmares about bears.

'Every child has bad dreams,' said the old woman. 'He's heard people talk of bears, and it's frightened him. He'll forget it as he grows older.'

But the idea of a bear coming into the house made

something move in Malyuta's memory, like a fish shifting and sending ripples through deep, deep water; and when Ambrosi continued to speak of the bear that came in the night, Malyuta asked the granny to make the child a little bag, filled with salt, to hang about his neck. Salt, Malyuta believed, would keep away witches and the bad spirits who haunt dreams.

When winter drew near again, and Malyuta knew that he would soon have to leave, he drew Ambrosi to him, and said, 'What shall I bring you when I come home again?'

Ambrosi stood between his father's hands, his cheeks glowing brightly under his dark hair, and then he said, 'A drum.'

Malyuta was surprised. 'Not sugar-bears? Not a little horse with a saddle and bridle?'

'A drum,' Ambrosi said.

So, that year, Malyuta risked his life by keeping some of the Czar's furs for himself. He sold them to a rich city peasant for money, and with the money in his pocket, he searched the city for the best toy drum to be had. He sloshed through the city's dark streets, through the snow that was being melted by the street-corner fires and the coming spring, and he searched the market stalls. There were wooden dolls, and wooden horses with carts to pull, and soldiers, and wooden chickens that pecked when you pulled a string. And there were drums, but none that were good enough for Malyuta's Ambrosi.

So he went to the city's beautiful shops, with their oil lamps shining through great glass windows, and the brightly-coloured, expensive toys and sweets inside. 'I want a toy drum,' he said. 'The best you have: a pretty one.' And he would tell the shopkeeper and the other customers of his Ambrusha: how beautiful he was, and how clever: 'The Czar has golden eggs and diamond flowers; but he has no treasure like my treasure! And I've promised him a drum.' It was as solemn a promise as any ever made over saint's bones. He wouldn't leave the city without the best drum he could buy.

Some were charmed by the big, rough-haired man's love of his child, and willingly clambered up ladders, delved behind counters, rummaged in back-rooms, to lay drums of all kinds before him; and also small castles, trumpets, and wooden bears who waved flags or beat drums of their own when strings were pulled.

There were those, too, who flinched at the stink of blood and badly cured skins that Malyuta brought with him, and disliked the way his big voice filled their shops and disturbed their wealthier customers. They answered coldly that all their drums were already on display, and that if none of them pleased him, they had no others to show. And when Malyuta had gone, taking his chatter of his perfect child with him, they said, 'Yes; and the toad thinks *his* children the most beautiful.'

The drum that Malyuta chose, at last, was just like the drums beaten by the soldiers of the Czar, except that it was small. Its skin was shining white: its round sides were of scarlet and glittering gold frogging; and it had blue ribbons and two beautifully turned little drum-sticks. Malyuta didn't think it good enough for Ambrosi, but it was the best in the city, and he paid the whole sum asked for it – but still had enough of his money left to buy a wooden horse from a market stall, and a little cart for it to pull. The horse and cart were what Malyuta would have wanted, if he had been Ambrosi. Then he hurried home to the village.

When he put the toys before Ambrosi, the little boy at once grabbed the horse and cart and hugged them to him. But he stared at the bright drum as if he didn't know what it was. Malyuta picked up one of the drumsticks and beat a rub-a-dub-dub on the drumskin.

Ambrosi picked up the other drumstick and stared at it. He tapped it twice on the drum, then dropped it and turned away to play with the horse and cart.

The old granny, seeing how disappointed Malyuta was, said, 'Never mind. He's only a baby and he'd forgotten that he'd asked for a drum. Look – he loves his horse and cart.'

Malyuta nodded, and would have thought no more on the matter if he had not, two days later, seen the scarlet drum lying outside the house door. Its golden frogging had been ripped off, and its white drumskin had been painted with red daubs. Malyuta picked it up and saw that the daubs were not as careless as they looked. There were signs that looked like deer's antlered heads, and suns, and men carrying spears, and houses, and fish and many, many other things. And, as he looked at these red signs painted on the white skin, something shifted once more, deep and cold, in the pool of his memory. For a moment he saw a picture in his mind: a picture that was hard to see and quick to vanish: the shape of man, dark against a brightly lit door, and, above the man's shoulder, the oval curve of a flat drum: a ghost drum. And later, he had seen the drum lying on the floor. Its skin had been painted with red signs. Malyuta frowned at the tickling memory. It was so dark and shifting that it was like the memory of a dream.

Ambrosi came running past, and Malyuta caught him in his arm. 'Did you paint these things on the drum?'

Ambrosi took a moment to forget whatever game he was playing. He looked at the red shapes on the drum. 'Yes, Daddy.' He turned into Malyuta's chest and tried to put his arms round him, but Malyuta was much too large.

'Why?'

'To make it like a real drum,' Ambrosi said.

'It is a real drum. It's just like the drums the Czar's soldiers use.'

'No. Like a real drum,' the little boy said.

'What is this red stuff?' Malyuta asked. 'What did you use?'

'Oh,' said the little boy, becoming excited and stammering. 'I got – got the – the bark – the bark from a tree. And I chew it – I chewed it up, and it goes, it goes red, and I used that. I can show you what tree if you want to make some.'

'Who taught you to do that?' Malyuta asked.

The little boy stopped chattering, and stared in front of him, as if he didn't know the answer to the question. 'Who showed you how?' Malyuta asked again.

'I just know,' said the little boy, giving up the puzzle.

Malyuta let him go, but he watched and listened to the boy more than before. And he noticed the songs that Ambrosi sang. No one else paid much attention to the chatter and singing of children. But Ambrosi sang songs that Malyuta had never heard before, and which weren't the tuneless chanting of children thinking that they have invented a song. It was no use, Malyuta learned, asking who had taught Ambrosi the song. Ambrosi didn't know.

And Ambrosi still had nightmares. While Malyuta was in the village, Ambrosi slept with him, and it was he who woke when the little boy began to cry in the night, and cuddled him until he was calmed. 'What did you dream?' he would ask, and the answer was always much the same.

'I dreamed a bear came in, and the bear wanted me to go with it.'

'The bear wanted you to go with it? How do you know?'

'Because it spoke to me. It told me to get up and come with it.'

'But you didn't go,' Malyuta said. 'You're safe here with me. And if that bear comes back, I'll kick its big hairy backside out of here.'

Then Ambrosi would begin to giggle, feeling safe snuggled with his father in the warm darkness, as long beams of midnight sunshine slanted through the shutters. Once he added, 'It told me a story.'

'The bear told you a story?'

'It always tells me a story. Then it says, "Get up and come with me." '

'What are the stories about?'

'Oh,' said Ambrosi, and sighed deeply. 'All things. Everything.' And he fell asleep again.

Malyuta lay awake, and raised his hand into a shaft of sunlight that fell over the bed. He felt the heat on his skin. Bears and midnight sunlight mingled in his mind and brought with them a memory of a stink so sharp that he truly smelled it again – a rank, bear stink. But while he struggled to sort dream from memory and waking from sleeping – he fell asleep, too.

When he woke, he remembered talking with

Ambrosi, and he worried about it for hours, until he said to the old granny, 'When I go hunting this year, I shall take Ambrusha with me.'

'He's a baby: much too young,' said the granny.

'I want him with me, to know that he's safe,' Malyuta said.

'Has any harm ever come to him while he's been with us?' said the granny. 'Do you say we don't look after our own daughter's son? Is this gratitude? And you want to take him amongst bears and wolves to be safe? Never while I breathe!'

And she became so angry, and the grandfather, and the aunts and uncles all became so angry, that Malyuta had to agree to leave Ambrosi behind.

It was not long before Malyuta was to leave that Ambrosi set his foot on the bench between Malyuta's legs and climbed into his father's lap. Settling himself comfortably, he said, 'Daddy; what is my real name?'

'Ambrosi! You know that it is.'

'No,' said Ambrosi. 'What is my *true* name?'

'I named you Ambrosi; that is your true name.'

Ambrosi said nothing, but stared at his father with the slightest of frowns, in the way he did when he didn't understand.

'Who has told you that Ambrosi isn't your real name?' Malyuta asked.

'The bear,' said the little boy, and Malyuta felt his bones fill with ice-water.

'The bear that comes in the night?' Ambrosi nodded. 'That bear is a dream, Ambrusha, a bad dream, not real. It doesn't matter what that bear says. Your name is Ambrosi.'

54

'Oh,' said the little boy. He climbed down from Malyuta's lap and ran away.

Before Malyuta went away that year, he asked the granny if she could manage to soak a little scrap of red cloth in holy water, and add it to the little package around Ambrosi's neck. Salt, and red, and holy water: that would surely keep him safe.

So (says the cat), the Earth turned and the leaves of my oak-tree died and fell about me with the acorns. Then came the snow, but my chain did not rust because it is gold. And next the snow melted, and the grass came, and Malyuta returned home with sweets and toys for Ambrosi.

'And does he still dream?' he asked the granny.

'No,' she said contentedly. 'No more bad dreams. He sleeps the night through now.'

'Do you still dream of the bear?' Malyuta asked his son.

'He's a man,' Ambrosi said.

'Who is a man?'

'The bear. He looks like a bear when he comes, but he's really a man.' The little boy clambered down from his father's lap, ran to a corner and brought back his drum. Its scarlet paint was scratched, the last of its gold frogging was gone, but the red signs painted on its white skin were still clear. 'I can play the drum. The bear shows me how.'

'The bear does?'

'And he teaches me songs.' Ambrosi leaned against his father and began to sing, in a voice so clear and tuneful that Malyuta was taken aback. The song had no words except 'Come, come, come and listen,' but those words were woven into a twisted tune that tickled the

55

ear and took odd, unexpected turns, so the listener could hardly wait for those notes to be repeated, to be sure of them. And the tune had sudden pauses, which made the listener hold his breath, caught in uncertainty, waiting for the music to begin again. And when Ambrosi ended the song, and laughed, Malyuta blinked and looked round and found that children had come in at the door to listen, that Granny had turned from her work and stood listening, that two dogs were lying attentively at his feet, their eyes fixed on Ambrosi, and that even the cat had left her warm sleeping place by the fire to creep closer.

'A beautiful song,' said Malyuta, and kissed his son, but felt dread in his bones. In his mind, raised again, was the picture of the darkened room and the man standing against bright midnight light, with the drum on his back and the bearskin hanging from his shoulders. He remembered, dimly, as if he was peering into darkness or squinting against a bright light. There had been a man's voice demanding, demanding – demanding Ambrosi.

'When I leave this year,' Malyuta said, 'I am taking Ambrusha with me.' But no, said the granny. No, said everyone. It would be foolish of him to hamper himself with a child. It might be the death of them both, out there, in the dark and cold. The child would grow up soon enough. Leave him in his mother's home a few years longer.

And so Malyuta again spent the winter alone; and when he returned in the spring, it seemed to him that the village was not the same as when he had left it, though he could not say why. But people looked at him oddly, as if they were a little afraid of him. They

56

pretended they had not seen him, so that they could hurry back into their houses without speaking to him. They did not seem to be as happy in their lives as he remembered. And when he asked the granny how his Ambrosi had been, she said, as she stirred the pot over the fire, 'He's a strange child.'

'What?' Malyuta said.

Still stirring, she said, 'He's not like my daughter.' This seemed strange to Malyuta, who remembered his wife by Ambrosi's face. 'And he's not like you, Malyuta.' She shook her head, moving her long wooden spoon round and round in the stew. 'My daughter never had such eyes . . . No, no, he's not like Yefrosinia. So who is he like?'

Ambrosi told stories. Malyuta would see him sitting in the dusty pathways that ran through the village, with other children gathered around him, and those other children would not move or speak until Ambrosi's story had ended. Malyuta liked to sit close by, if he could, and listen, and watch the faces of Ambrosi's listeners. It made him proud. But he noticed that other adults would see the children, and would frown, and would go widely around them – but if ever a man or woman strayed close enough to hear Ambrosi's words, then they would stay and listen to the end too.

In the evening, when people were gathered on the benches outside the granny's house, the whole company, men, women and children, would fall silent and listen if Ambrosi began to tell a story, or to sing. But sometimes, as soon as he began, the granny would cry out sharply, 'You have told enough stories today, Ambrosi!' Or some man would clap his hands together loudly and say, 'The old speak, the young listen!' Then

Ambrosi would break off his story and, though the children were disappointed, the adults seemed relieved.

Round went the year again, down into darkness and rising into light; and when Malyuta returned to the village that spring, he had hardly finished greeting everyone, when the granny put her hands on her hips and said to him, 'Malyuta, when you go away this year, you must take Ambrosi with you.'

'What? Do you think him old enough to travel with me at last?'

'No,' said the granny, 'but we don't want him here any more. You must take him away.'

'What has he done?' Malyuta asked.

'He tells stories,' said the old woman. 'He sings songs.'

'Is that wrong?'

'He tells stories that no one has ever told him. He sings songs that we have never heard.'

Malyuta laughed. 'Well! He's a clever boy, my Ambrusha! He makes them up.'

'No child so young could make up such stories,' said the old woman. 'Such long stories, such strange ideas – ! And never a word out of place or forgotten.'

'And if you start listening,' said an aunt, 'then you must listen to the end, no matter what there is to be done. The children want to listen to him all the time!'

'My Yefrosinia never had such eyes,' said the old woman.

'He puts a spell on you,' said the aunt.

'Ah, what women's nonsense!' Malyuta said.

That made the old woman angry, and she said, 'Well, you will find it's men's nonsense too, because we have all agreed – you must take your son away! If he is your son and not a change-child!'

'I shall take him away!' Malyuta said. 'I shall take him away now!' And he called Ambrosi, and began to gather together all the boy's things, and his own, and load them onto his reindeer. He expected the old grandmother and grandfather to panic at the idea of Ambrosi being taken away from them so soon, but they watched the packing without saying anything. 'I shall take my food to another village!' Malyuta said, but still no one asked him to stay. It was true what the granny had said: the whole village wanted Ambrosi to go.

Ambrosi cried at being taken away from his home, and in the new village, he told no stories and sang no songs. Nor did he wake in the night with bad dreams. 'Do you still dream of the bear?' Malyuta asked him, and Ambrosi nodded. 'What does the bear say to you these days?'

'He says no one will ever want to hear my stories, or want me to live with them, and I should tell him my true name and go with him.'

Then Malyuta hugged Ambrosi as tightly as the bear could have done, and said, '*I* want to hear your stories! *I* want you to live with me. You must not listen to the bear!'

When winter came that year Malyuta could not leave Ambrosi with people who were still strangers, and so Ambrosi was seven years old when he began spending the long winter darkness with his father, hunting and killing for fur.

Ambrosi knew the summer, when he fell asleep and woke up to the same bright light: he knew the paths deep in dry white dust, the thick greenery of the trees, the bird song. But all he knew of winter was firelight and house-warmth, and the safe darkness of the back yard.

Now his father took him into a wilderness of deep, silent snow, eerie, snow-lit darkness and cold. There was no sound but the wind which moaned in his ear and then travelled on and on, and on, into emptiness and darkness, perhaps to moan at the ear of a lynx or wolf, but not at the ear of any other boy. The loneliness, the space, was glorious and dizzying.

During the summer, Malyuta had made Ambrosi his own small bow and arrows, and his own small skis: the ski for the right foot being twice as long as the ski for the left. He strapped them to Ambrosi's feet and showed him how to use them, pushing with the short ski and skimming over the snow on the long ski, pushing himself along with the bow. Ambrosi learned quickly, but pushing always with the same leg was tiring and he was soon worn out. Then Malyuta wrapped him in a reindeer skin and put him on top of the sled pulled by a reindeer which still had its skin. There Ambrosi would sit, scudding along between the white land and the black sky, watching his father fly over the snow far ahead and circle back to him, his dogs following.

When they reached Malyuta's hunting grounds, Malyuta set up his camp and, after resting, slung snares on his back and set off, on skis, to study the country and find the best places for his traps. Ambrosi was left behind in the tent, with a big, thick-maned, blue-eyed dog to guard him. Malyuta knew that the dog would stay with the little boy and protect him, as a young thing in need of protection, as fiercely as it would protect a puppy.

Alone, and with many an anxious thought of his son,

Malyuta made his way through the snow-light, observing paw prints and droppings, and learning from them the best places to set his traps. Then he flew back over the snow to his camp, and found Ambrosi awake and playing noisily with the dog. Malyuta picked him up and shook him. 'When I leave you, you must keep quiet – quiet as a little bird when its mother leaves the nest. If you make a noise, wolves will come, and worse – bears will come. The good old dog won't be able to save you from a bear. The white bear isn't afraid of dogs, or you, or me, or the Czar and all his armies! The bear will eat you!'

When they were warm in the tent, with the fire giving them light, Malyuta made Ambrosi drink two bowls of thick caravan tea, with reindeer butter added to it, to make sure that he had enough inside him to keep him warm. 'If a bear ever does come while I am away,' Malyuta said, 'then you must keep still, still as you can. Don't make a sound. Don't run away – a bear can run faster than you can! But if you keep quiet and still, it may think you are already dead and go by.'

When Malyuta hunted wolf, he didn't carry bow and arrows with him, but a long, iron-sheathed staff and a strong knife. For mile after mile he would skim over the snow, through the icy twilight, pushing with his right foot and the staff, gliding forward on his left foot, following the tracks of the wolves.

The pack, when they knew he followed them, would scatter, but Malyuta would choose one, a young healthy wolf with a fine coat. The wolf would stretch its legs and its lungs and run over the frozen snow, under the black sky, but behind it would come Malyuta.

And, when the wolf tired, it would turn to fight its

61

tormentor. But Malyuta had no teeth to match a wolf's. He would glide past on his skis and, as he passed the wolf, he would strike it hard across the back with his iron-shod staff. If he struck right, he would break the wolf's back, and it would fall to the snow, half-paralysed. Then Malyuta would kill it with his knife.

He would rip off its skin, bundle up the bloody thing and strap it to his back. Sometimes, as he skied away, he would hear the mourning song of the living wolves for the dead one: the whole wolf-pack singing the ghost-song that would guide the dead wolf to the Ghost World. He would mourn with them, knowing they felt as he had felt when his wife had died. 'You kill for food,' he called to the singing wolves. 'So do I. The Czar, my master, won't allow me to live unless I bring him your skins.'

When Malyuta was away, Ambrosi had to learn not to be afraid. There was no sunrise or sunset to tell him how long his father had been gone, or to give hope that he might return soon. It was always dark.

Ambrosi had to learn to trust that Malyuta would come back: that no matter how long his absence seemed, no matter how frightened and lonely Ambrosi became, that Malyuta would come back. When he was hungry, he knew where the strips of dried reindeer meat and the dried fish were. He would eat them, and share them with his blue-eyed dog. When he was bored, he would put on his skis and practise the use of them; or practise with his bow and arrows. Or he would run and jump in the snow, tussle with the dog that ran leaping after him, and throw snowballs for the dog to chase. He forgot Malyuta's warnings until the time when the dog growled and cowered to the snow. Ambrosi looked round and saw a dim grey starless shape against the black, starred sky. It was a bear, a white bear, come to look at them.

Ambrosi sank down in the snow beside the cowering dog, and was afraid. His heart beat faster and faster as he remembered everything his father had said about the bears: their curiosity, their strength, their hunger, their speed. The dog growled again, and Ambrosi pulled it to him and held its muzzle. He didn't look away from the bear. If it was going to eat him, he wanted to see it coming.

The bear sat quietly and looked at him. It didn't move its head about and sway, as Malyuta said bears did when they were angry. After a long, cold while, it raised one paw to its head, as if it was going to wave. It didn't wave – it pushed its own head off. And there was another head under the bear's head: a man's head, with long hair and a beard. And the skin of the bear's body split and parted like a cloak, and there was a man sitting on the snow, in a tunic and trousers and boots and mittens.

Ambrosi squinted, to be sure of what he was seeing, because the snow threw up wavering mists of light into the darkness that shifted shapes. And, squinting, he was sure that what he saw was a bear; but if he moved his head slightly – and he only dared to move slightly – then he saw the man.

The man moved and pushed back one side of his cloak, uncovering something with a round edge that was strapped to his back. The man seemed to smile – it was hard to see in the darkness – and then tapped the thing strapped to his back. There rang out in the dark, cold emptiness the sound of a drum!

The man stood and pressed his forefinger against his

lips. He drew his cloak around him, lifted the bear's head onto his own head – and there was a white bear, unmistakably a white bear standing on its hind legs. It dropped onto all fours and strode away into the snow-haze.

It was a long, long time before Malyuta returned, with a wolf skin. Ambrosi told him nothing of the bear, because the man beneath the bear's skin had told him to say nothing, and because Malyuta would be angry that Ambrosi had made a noise to attract the bear to their camp.

Often Malyuta took Ambrosi with him, to visit the traps he had set. He wanted Ambrosi to learn to ski well, and to learn how to set a trap, and how to skin an animal. When they returned from those journeys, Ambrosi was exhausted, by the exercise and by the cold. He would drop into a deep sleep, as far below dreams as a stone in the deep sea is below the waves. He had no dreams of bears.

When the winter was nearly over, Ambrosi hoped that they might return to his granny's village, but first they went to the city – a terrifying place – and then they went to a village of strangers, where Malyuta asked for shelter in the Czar's name, and offered to pay for lodgings with a share of the food he had earned for his furs.

Malyuta kept Ambrosi busy through the summer: he must learn how skis were made and repaired, and the making of bows and arrows. He must learn how to keep the sleds and harness in good trim, and the care of the reindeer. He must learn what stores they would need to take with them, and how to load the sled; and he must practise with his bow, and practise, and practise, and practise. With all this, and the chores their hosts expected of them, there was little time for story-telling, even if Ambrosi had wanted to tell his stories to strangers.

Winter came again, and this winter Malyuta worked Ambrosi harder. He was expected to ski out to inspect the traps with his father, and never to whine that he was tired or cold. He must choose the places to set snares, and learn whether he chose wisely or not by his catch. He must try, with his bow, to shoot sables; and he must try his hand at skinning, rolling the fur off the bloody flesh as a mother might roll a tight sock off a child's foot. Whenever their catch was a sable, Malyuta would say, 'Cheeks as red as blood, skin white as snow, hair black as sable,' and dab Ambrosi's nose with his bloodied fingers.

When they needed rest, or when the weather was bad, they would stay in their tent, and build up the fire until the small space was hot and smoky, and filled with panting dogs until it was hotter still, and they were able to take off much of their heavy clothing. Then they would eat, and Malyuta would tell stories. He would tell Ambrosi of Yefrosinia, his dead mother; and of wolf-hunts, and of those fierce animals, the gluttons, who have no fear, and no sense, and will eat anything.

'Their eyes are bigger than their bellies. They don't know that reindeer are too big for them, so they wait until the reindeer is eating, then they creep up and grab it by the throat. And when they've killed it, they eat it and eat it and eat it, the gluttons, until they stuff themselves to death! But sometimes, they'll drag their big bellies away to where two trees grow close together. Then they squeeze themselves between the two trees and squeeze themselves empty! Then they go looking for another reindeer – or a bear.'

'A bear?' Ambrosi said, remembering the white bear that had come and looked at him, and had turned to a man.

'Gluttons are too stupid to be scared and they think only of eating. They don't know that they can't kill a bear. If they see a bear, they'll chase him, as if they were a lynx after a hare, and they'll jump on him!'

'And what happens?'

'The bear gives them one swipe, and then eats *them*. Only stupid gluttons and men chase the bear.'

Malyuta told of beavers, and of how the beaver, though a clever animal, is so madly fond of aspen bark that when it sees a piece it becomes as stupid as the glutton and will enter any trap to get it. 'But the beavers are like men and women,' said Malyuta, thinking of his dead wife. 'They fall in love, and they marry, and they live with one another all their lives long. When a beaver dies, its wife or its husband will pine away and die too. And when one beaver is caught in a trap, it calls out for its mate, or its children, and its family comes and they bite through the trap, or open it – and so the hunter finds his trap empty or broken! But who can blame the beavers for that?' Malyuta would ask, as he hugged Ambrosi even closer to his side within the warmth of the reindeer skin. 'If my Ambrusha was caught in a trap, wouldn't I do anything to get him out? Wouldn't I bite down walls with my teeth, bash my way through with my head, make myself a bridge, a ladder, a boat, a sled for him to escape? Surely I would. So I am always glad – though this is between us and I want no one else to know of it – I am always glad when I find my beaver-traps empty.'

Sometimes, instead of Malyuta telling a story, Ambrosi would tell one. He told old stories, that he could have learned from his granny, but he told them so well that Malyuta would listen, fascinated, but afraid. And Ambrosi told stories that Malyuta had never heard before: long, complicated stories that Malyuta could not remember once they had ended – but Ambrosi had every turn of the tale, all in order, and every word was confident and sure. Malyuta felt himself drifting into the words, and had to shake himself to remember that he was a father listening to the chatter of his small son.

There were songs in many of the stories, and Ambrosi sang them in a strong clear voice, each note true; and the dogs would press closer to him and lay their big heads in his lap, their blue eyes fixed on him.

Where did this gift for music and words come from? Malyuta had no such gifts himself, and neither had Yefrosinia. It both frightened and disappointed him that his son should be so different from himself. Often, if Ambrosi began a song or story, Malyuta would hurriedly begin one of his own before Ambrosi's words could cast their spell over him, and make him forget that he was the father, the elder, the man who should talk while Ambrosi listened. He was sometimes ashamed of himself for this, but Ambrosi's story-telling made him feel so uneasy that he preferred the shame to the fear.

As I walk round my tree (says the cat) it shelters me from the sun and rain with a thick roof of gold-green leaves. It flowers; it fruits. It drops yellow leaves thickly around me and lets the rain fall on me; it drops acorns. It adds another year's thickness to its trunk. And as my tree grows older, so Ambrosi grew older and stronger, year by year. And there came a year when, as they started off into the snow for their hunt, Malyuta thought that, as this was the beginning of a new year, he would take a new look at things. And he looked at his son, and saw that Ambrosi was as tall as himself.

A tall son whose hair, lashes, brows were as black as a sable's coat. His skin was pale against the darkness. Red blood glowed lively in his face. As tall as his father, and strong, and altogether beautiful.

What was listening, Malyuta thought, with dread, when I made that wish over the dead sable? Why am I chosen for my dearest wish to come true?

And yet, seeing clearly in that moment, Malyuta saw that the old granny had been right: Ambrosi was not at all like Yefrosinia or himself.

There was no need to warn Ambrosi not to whine now: he could outrun Malyuta on skis, and he burned with such inward heat that he seemed not to notice the cold. He could kill a sable with a blunt arrow that didn't spoil its coat; he could dodge the teeth of a fox caught in a trap and kill it in a moment, and skin it in a moment more. But it was on this trip that he said to his father, 'We must be careful about cooking. A bear is following us.'

Ambrosi's sleep was no longer the deep, deep sleep of exhaustion. Now he dreamed again.

4

In the continual dark of winter, in the continual light of summer, the cat walks round and round the tree, and the golden chain is wound up, link by link.

Do you remember the people Kuzma turned into wolves (asks the cat)?

Now I shall tell what became of them.

When the shaman had gone, the wolves-who-had-been-people came back to their camp, back to the whimpering cubs and the burning tents. The camp-dogs, bewildered, barked at them, until the wolves ran away. But the wolves always returned, until they realized that there was nothing in their camp that they could use any more. They had paws, not hands. The tents, the sleds, the tools, the clothes, were all useless to them.

Then the wolf who had been White Reindeer picked up one of the cubs in her mouth and started away across the snow, to find some place sheltered from the killing wind. The other females, and some of the males, picked up cubs in their mouths and trotted after her, while others drove away the snapping dogs, or stayed to guard the cubs who could not be carried away yet.

White Reindeer found an outcrop of rock, which had been blown partly clear of snow by the wind, and in whose crevices there was shelter and warmth. But a wolf can carry only one cub at a time, and when the adult wolves returned to fetch the cubs they had left behind, they found their guards howling. The guards had not been able to keep off a lynx, nor the freezing wind, and the cubs were dead.

In silence the wolves returned over the snow to the rocks where the cubs they had saved, and their adult guards, waited. The guardian wolves came out to meet them, sniffing for the cubs they should have brought. The returning wolves had no words to explain what had happened. But the wolf that had been White Reindeer lifted up her head and howled, so that all the wolves gathered there should know what had been lost. Within moments all the wolves had lifted their heads and were howling too. Their cold, cold cries rose into the darkness, each cry weaving its own way among the others, and seeming to call down the black sky and nail it to the frozen earth.

The wolf who had been Bitten-by-a-Fox suddenly choked and broke off his song. Another of the wolves had run at him, snapping, threatening to bite. Again the wolf ran at him, and another joined in, snapping at Bitten-by-a-Fox's ears. Fox didn't fight back. Cringing close to the snow, his tail low, he crept away from them until they stopped chasing him; and then he lay on the snow with his nose on his paws. He had threatened the shaman with a knife; he had brought down the curse on them. He deserved to be driven away. The dead cubs were dead because of his fault. Guilt and shame, and sorrow for all they had lost filled him until he ached with the fullness of it, and he longed to howl it out. But the other wolves did not want him to join his voice to their song. He could only whimper.

That night the wolves slept in the shelter of the rocks where they lay close by the cubs, keeping them warm. One or two, on guard, lay outside, huddled together. Only Bitten-by-a-Fox was alone, lying at a distance, his fur lifted and ruffled by the cold wind. But soon two old wolves left the shelter of the rocks and loped down the hill to him. They licked his face and ears and lay down on either side of him. They were Bone Hook, his father, and White Reindeer, his mother.

The wolves-who-had-been-people had a hard time of it that winter. They had to feed themselves, but had no practice in hunting as wolves. The reindeer they had once followed and fed on, now ran from them, and kicked them when they came close. The smaller game was hard to find and harder to catch, with only teeth to replace snares and traps. More of the cubs died, from cold and hunger. Real wolf-cubs are not born in the worst of winter: it was a terrible curse Kuzma had laid on them. The people tried to sing the ghost-song they would have sung for dead children, telling the children's spirits how to follow the path that would lead them to safety in the Ghost World – but their singing was the ghost-singing of wolves. And were they mourning for lost, dead children, or for wolf-cubs? Bitten-by-a-Fox, lying away from the other wolves, and not allowed to join the singing, trembled with the sorrow that filled him and could not be spilled. A wolf cannot weep.

The adult wolves were thin and weak, and some sickened, and lay down and died. It is a fierce pain, the pain of seeing a loved friend suffer, when you can offer no relief or help. The wolves who survived went back to the camp they had made as people. They fought with the few half-starved dogs who were still there; they ate the reindeer hide of the tents and sled covers; they dragged out the stores of dried fish and meat, and gnawed on them. Bitten-by-a-Fox hung back, at the edges of the pack, and ran in to snatch a mouthful here and there. Most of the other wolves still snapped at him and drove him away whenever he came near. When every hungry, miserable moment reminded them of what he had brought on them, it was hard to forgive him.

But only change is everlasting, and even such winters as this long northern winter must change, in time, to spring. Days began to break the long night: short, bleak days of a few hours' length, quickly dimming into twilight and night again. But even in that weak, brief light the shape of the wolf sitting at look-out above the den would seem to waver – was it a wolf, or a man, who sat there?

The days grew longer, and the snow melted, and the streams filled and ran fast – and the wolves were people again for hours at a time. As soon as they looked at each other and saw human faces, they began to call each other's names and to talk. They talked even as they hurried to their old camp, to search the abandoned sleds and ruined tents for clothes, which they brought back to the wolf-den and hid, against the time when there would be no night.

And summer did come. The sun rose and, even at midnight, the sky was white with its light. So few of the people were left that there were enough clothes rescued from the old camp to dress them all. They embraced each other: they stroked down each other's backs, touched each other's faces, admired each other's long, straight legs. Never had their human shapes seemed so beautiful. They gathered at their old camp, where no dogs prowled any more, to plan what they would do next – but instead of planning, they talked. They remembered everything that had happened to them as wolves, and retold it in human words: they remembered and retold all their old stories, thankful that they had not forgotten them. During all this, Bitten-by-a-Fox sat aside and listened to the tongues making words again but – hard though it was – he kept silent himself. The people had made it clear to him, by angry looks, that he was no more welcome in human shape than he had been as a wolf.

'We must find our reindeer again,' some were saying. 'We must go up into the mountains: that's where they'll be.'

'I am soon to give birth,' said a woman. 'Will I have a child or a wolf-cub? I am frightened,' she said, and the woman nearest her hugged her and held her, but could not answer her question.

'At least the children born in summer will have enough to eat,' said White Reindeer, 'if we can find our herd.'

Bone Hook said, 'Our tools are broken and scattered. We will have to make new ones, repair the sleds – and we have no dogs to help us.'

From his place aside, Bitten-by-a-Fox spoke up then. He spoke quietly and to his father, knowing that no one else would listen to him. 'Father, it's no use to follow the reindeer. Even if we had our dogs and tools, we would be high in the mountain when the winter and darkness begins again. We would turn to wolves. How could we travel down from the mountains then? Our reindeer

73

would run from us. How could we carry the babies? How would we manage the sleds?'

Bone Hook nodded; but the others were angry. Some threw pieces of broken tools. 'He brought the curse on us,' cried one woman. 'He should be made to keep his mouth shut!'

'He should be sent away,' said someone else.

'Yes,' said another. 'He always had his sweet words ready when he wanted to persuade us to do as he wanted. But where were they when the shaman came?'

Bitten-by-a-Fox sat cross-legged on the ground and held his head low, saying nothing.

Bone Hook said, 'I ask you to remember when the shaman came. Remember what the shaman was like, and what was said – '

'It was what was done!' a man shouted. 'He threatened a shaman with a knife!'

'He was trying to save the children!' Bone Hook said. 'He tried to talk sweetly to the shaman: don't you remember how the shaman answered? Nothing would have saved us from the curse. No, I won't ask my son to go away. Any of you who don't want his company can leave – and see what kind of welcome you get among other people when winter comes and you turn to wolves!'

This made the people angry and they all shouted out against Fox. One man's voice rose above them all. 'Bone Hook, if you weren't his father, you would agree. If he was another man's son, you would be the first to say he should go.'

Bitten-by-a-Fox came over to stand beside his mother and father. 'I think you must go south, Father,' he said, 'to where the people live in houses, and grow rye in

74

fields. You can hunt, and you can work for the farmers – '

'Work for farmers!' shouted Leaf indignantly. 'Run about and do what we're told by men who sit by the fire all winter?'

'If you have a better idea, tell it to us,' Bone Hook said; and he was told, by many, that they should follow their lost reindeer herd.

Argument broke out again, with some reminding others that the reindeer were far away, and they had no dogs to help find them and must, in any case, prepare for their winter change to wolves.

'Well, what will happen if we change to wolves among the Southern farmers?' a woman demanded. 'They'll hunt us down and kill us!'

All the while this argument had been going on, Bitten-by-a-Fox had been quietly going about the ruined camp, gathering things into a hide bag. Dried fish and meat from one of the sleds that had not been entirely robbed by bears or the wolf-people themselves; bone needles and sinew-thread, a knife.

'At least in the south there will be cows and goats and chickens,' someone said.

'And arrows and spears!' said someone else.

Bone Hook saw that his son was packing for a journey, and went over to him. 'Where are you going?' he asked.

'To find the shaman who set this curse on us, and ask him to remove it,' Bitten-by-a-Fox said, and bent to pick up a belt from the ground.

Bone Hook took him by the arms, pulled him upright and held him. 'A shaman isn't found by looking,' he said. 'A shaman comes when he wishes to be found, and only then. You must stay with us: so many died in the

75

winter that we need everyone, whatever we decide to do.'

'It's my fault that so many died,' Bitten-by-a-Fox said. 'They want me to go away, and I should go away.'

'The shaman meant us harm when he first came. Whatever you had said or done, it would have ended the same.'

'No,' Bitten-by-a-Fox said. 'I should have kept quiet and let you talk for us, Father. There will be nothing but ill-feeling and arguments while I stay.'

Bone Hook knew that was true. 'Well then,' he said. 'Let me ask your brothers to go with you. You shouldn't go alone.'

'My brothers have their families – what is left of them,' Fox said. Both his brothers had lost cubs, or children, in the winter. 'I am no fool, Father, for all I made the shaman angry. I shall come to no harm. But it's best if I go away – and if I can find the shaman, then some good may come of it.'

Bone Hook couldn't deny the truth of this. He put his arms around Bitten-by-a-Fox and hugged him hard, already feeling the painful loss of this living son. 'Next summer,' he said, 'when we have this shape again, those of us who are still alive will be here. Come to us then, if you can.'

'I will,' Bitten-by-a-Fox said; and then he took his bag and walked away. The people watched him go, and some of them looked about at the others, as if they were looking for someone who would call Fox back. But others put their hands on their hips and said, 'Good: we are well rid of that bad-luck bringer.'

Still, each passing day brought more thoughts of all the dangers there were in the world for one man alone –

one very young man – a boy, to tell the truth – a boy who was strong and clever, but had never known what it was like to be without the help and advice of his mother and aunts and sisters, his father and brothers and uncles. When it was too late, when Bitten-by-a-Fox was out of sight and gone, then the people began to feel keenly that he might never come back to them; and they had to keep telling themselves that he had brought the curse down on them, and that they were glad he was gone.

Bone Hook and White Reindeer, and Fox's brothers and sisters, said nothing about his going at all.

Where did Bitten-by-a-Fox go? He went shaman-hunting over the grasslands and through the forests of the North. He made himself a bow and arrows, and with them he shot fish, and birds and hare; and he scanned the wide country for houses that travel on feet. He saw none. Shamans are not found unless they want to be.

So, as the short summer hurried by, Bitten-by-a-Fox made his slow way to the little villages, and he asked there of witches and shamans. He was not made welcome. The villagers knew by his broad-boned face and long eyes, by his way of speaking and his clothes, that he was one of the reindeer people. The villagers did not like the reindeer people. They looked at Bitten-by-a-Fox from their doorways and windows, careful not to get near him. They thought him dirty. They feared that he knew all kinds of magic and had brought bad luck to their houses. They thought him stupid because he could not say their words easily. They shut their doors on him. They said to him, 'We're asking you nicely – go away.'

So he kept clear of the farming villages, and made his way into the mountains, because he knew that it was in the mountains that he would meet with his own people.

And he came to a settlement of little wooden houses among the trees. He knew by the storehouses raised on long poles that these were houses of the reindeer people. They didn't follow the reindeer from place to place with all their families and belongings, as his own family did, but he knew that he would be welcome among them.

And so he was, for his speech, his face and his clothes made him known as a friend, just as they made him known as an enemy to the farmers. He was invited to stay at the first house he called at, and people quickly came from the other houses to meet him. He gave them news of his own family, and listened to news of theirs; but when he was asked why he was travelling alone, he said that he wanted to see something of the world. He mentioned nothing of Kuzma's curse.

He stayed for days with the mountain people, paying for his food with work, and he kept his eyes and ears open. He heard a woman ask an old man if he would make a medicine for her child, who wasn't eating as he should. So then Bitten-by-a-Fox went to the old man and asked him, 'Are you a witch?'

The old man laid a hand on Bitten-by-a-Fox's arm and said, 'I am. But, another time, don't ask so bluntly. Don't you know that the Christians burn witches? Instead, ask, 'Are you one of the wise?' Or, 'Do you know the old ways?'

'I'm sorry, Grandfather. My people live so far from everyone, we have no need to call old things by new names. If you are one of the wise, Grandfather, I need your advice.'

'Any help I can give you, I will,' said the old man.

'I need to find a shaman, Grandfather.'

'Not an easy thing; or a wise thing,' said the old witch, and looked carefully into Bitten-by-a-Fox's face, until Fox looked away. 'I am a witch,' said the old man. 'I can doctor, and I know a little of the three magics. I have even seen the Ghost World Gate in a dream, though I have never dared go through it. But I – I would never seek out a shaman. They are best left alone.'

'But I must find this shaman, Grandfather. I must ask a favour of him.'

'Why?' the old man asked; but Bitten-by-a-Fox looked at the ground and wouldn't tell. Even though these people were his people, and his friends, he feared to tell them what he would become when dark nights began to split summer into days. He feared that their friendship would turn to a simple wish to kill him. The more he thought of the words he would need to tell of the curse, the more he knew that he could never speak them. He said only, 'I must, Grandfather, I must.'

The old man put his hand on Bitten-by-a-Fox's arm again, but this time gripped tighter. 'Shamans cannot be reached unless they wish it. They can see you, hear you, smell you before you ever come near them; they can escape from you into other worlds. Forget shamans, boy, whatever you want with them. Go back to your own people and be happy with the life you have there.'

Bitten-by-a-Fox didn't say that there was no happy life for his people any more; and he left that place soon after. Since he had found no help in the country villages, nor among his own people, he travelled to a Southern town, a place where many, many houses were crowded together: a place that seemed as packed and full as his father's tent, but which was neither comfortable nor friendly. It stank, it reeked, it hummed, of people's

79

clothes and people's breath, and people's rubbish; and it clanged, it clamoured with their noise; and no matter where he turned or looked, he saw a wall.

It was hard for Bitten-by-a-Fox to live in the town, but at least the townspeople cared less about his speech, the shape of his face, and his clothes than the country people had. The townspeople called him 'Lapp – Numbskull – Lappie', but they didn't always mean harm by it; and as long as he had money, they weren't going to chase him away. Many strange foreigners came to the town, and the townspeople were no longer frightened by them. They laughed at Fox's tall cap, and they said his mother was a reindeer, but Fox liked them better than the villagers. 'My mother is a White Reindeer,' he said.

He earned money by running errands about the town, and by setting snares for rabbits in the countryside close by. He spent the money on cheap food and lodgings and on anything he heard about that might take Kuzma's curse from his people. All the time he watched the summer sky for the first night of winter.

He bought a candle from a witch because, she said, burning the candle would remove any bad influence that hung over him or threatened him. He had to go without food for a day, to have enough money to buy the candle. It was green and, when burned, gave off a smell of old mutton fat burning in a fire. The others who slept in the room he lodged in complained, and coughed, and held their noses, but Bitten-by-a-Fox burned the candle until it burned out. Then he thought: How can I know if it's worked until winter comes? How can I be sure?

So he found another witch, who sold him a talisman to hang round his neck, a talisman that would guard him from all evil spells. But once it was hanging round his neck, he thought: Even if it works, it will only work for me and not for all my people.

So he bought, from another witch, some powdered leaves. He spooned some into a pot and brewed a tea. He drank it all, though its taste wasn't good. The rest of the leaves he packed away carefully and carried in his pocket, to give to the rest of his people, when he should meet them again. He felt no different for drinking the tea, and couldn't tell if it had broken the curse.

And now the brightness of the summer sky was dimming into short twilit evenings. There was, as yet, no such darkness as could be called a night; but the nights were coming.

Before they came Bitten-by-a-Fox bought a bag made of waxed cloth, and left the town. He camped in the countryside, and waited. As the twilights deepened, he took off his clothes, hid them and the bag, and waited again.

He hoped that the burning of the candle had freed him. He hoped that wearing the talisman would guard him; he hoped that drinking the leaf-tea had broken the spell – but the words of Kuzma's curse rose with the sun and spoke in the darkness. The first hour of true night changed him into a wolf. Change is everlasting.

When daylight returned him to his own shape, he found his clothes again, put them on, and began travelling. He was afraid to stay in the South country, where the farmers hunted wolves. He would return to the far, cold North, where the hunters were few, and of his own people.

He travelled as far as he could by day, in his human shape, often begging or buying a ride on a cart. But he always left all human company before darkness, and found some hiding place where he could strip off his clothes and hide them, ready for his change to wolf. The further north he travelled, the longer and darker the nights became, and the shorter and dimmer the days. Soon, there would be no daylight, and he would lose his human shape, his human tongue and words.

As he travelled closer to the North, and his time as a man became shorter, a great anger grew in him. He remembered those who had called him stupid and dirty because he wasn't of their people, who had chased him away, called him thief and refused to help him. He remembered the witch of his own people who had told him to go back to his family and be happy, because there was no way of finding a shaman. He remembered the townspeople, who had tricked money from him for useless spells that hadn't lifted the curse, and who had jeered at his clothes and his family. Tricksters and liars, all. Soon he couldn't stop to buy bread from a house, or hear a passer-by call to him, without a rage of sickness rising. The smell of these people: how greasy and reeking of their fat it was! How it made his mouth water and his stomach sick! Their breath: how it told of the grain and vegetables they'd munched, to sweeten their flesh. How their shrilling, moaning voices stung his ear; how he felt himself tremble if one seemed about to touch him. The wolf in him was rising to the dark, and he began to keep from houses and farm-lands. When he saw people, he wanted to run, or snarl and bite, so it was better not to see them at all.

Snow had already fallen, and the nights were growing so long that he was left only a few hours of daylight, and even those hours were greying into twilight. In another few days, even the twilit hours would vanish. He began to pack his clothes in the waxed bag and bury them before his change, in a place he marked and remembered, because he never knew which would be the night when no morning came, and he remained a wolf.

It came, that long night. Then he was a wolf, alone, until winter's end.

Some things are told easily (says the cat); some things can hardly be told at all. If I speak of how long and cold that winter was, no hearer or reader of my words feels the cold growing harder and deeper, until it squeezes, and crushes the blood from fingers which turn blue and white. No; my words are spoken in a moment, and then are gone. My hearers don't live in my words as Bitten-by-a-Fox lived in darkness, and only darkness; half-blinded by darkness when he was waking, and followed into his dreams by darkness when he slept; living in darkness until he felt the ever-dark sky like a weight on his back. The moon swelled full and melted the darkness to a mist of snow-reflected light; then dwindled and left the world to glimmer with mere starlight . . . Moon after moon, and still the darkness and the cold continued.

Bitten-by-a-Fox forgot that there had ever been warmth or light. He was alone, without the comfort of family or pack around him. He couldn't hunt large game, and had to chase snow-rabbits, ermine and ptarmigan, and often enough he was robbed of what he caught by the wolf-pack that truly owned the land he hunted. But he couldn't move on to hunt other land, because he had left his human clothes buried in their waxed bag, and when spring came – distantly remembered spring! – he would need those clothes. Even spring is cold.

83

Never, through all that long winter, was Bitten-by-a-Fox without the feeling of hunger in his belly. Never could he rest calmly, without fearing that the other wolves would come on him, or steal from him. Sometimes, when he heard these wolves announcing their presence to the moon, their music falling and echoing across the snow-filled land, he would find long cries pulled from his own throat, cries of anger and sorrow, and longing, longing, longing for the day when the sun would rise and shine on him, in his man's shape, for even a single hour.

But change is everlasting. However trapped we seem, however endlessly it seems we must endure, change comes – though not always the change we wish. The night of winter was greyed to twilight and, at last, there was a minute, two minutes, three, of true daylight.

Bitten-by-a-Fox made his way back to where he had buried his clothes and scratched up the bag that held them with his wolf's nails. Soon he had his hour of daylight, and longer. He began travelling north again, travelling as far as he could while the light lasted; and eating and sleeping in the shape of a wolf.

When he reached the place where he was to meet his people, the snow had melted, and the full white light of summer had washed the sky. The people were gathered together to wait for him, as they had said they would. They even had a few tents, which they must have made, or repaired during the summer, and then hidden against the time when they would need them.

He knew when they had seen him, because they left their tents and their fires and came walking and running to meet him. And when he saw them running to him, despite the dread in him at what they would say to him, he ran to reach them the sooner. The people caught him, and hugged and held him in strong arms, and passed him to the arms of latecomers, and they kissed him, every one of them, men and women, and held the children up to hug and kiss him. They were, every one of them, his uncles and aunts and cousins and brothers and sisters, by marriage if not by blood. For a long year they had been thinking of him, all alone and far out of reach of their help; and they had been dreading how they would feel if this summer passed and he did not come back to them. So now they were dizzy and drunk with the pleasure and relief of his return.

Bitten-by-a-Fox was dizzy himself, and laughed aloud at finding himself welcomed and no longer blamed. He was relieved that the smell of these beloved people, the taste of their skin on his lips when he kissed them, didn't make him want to bite. Among them, he was fully human, and no wolf.

But he had been looking among them all for one missing face, and expecting to see that face as they came closer and closer to the tents. 'Where is Bone Hook?' he asked his mother, White Reindeer, and, when she didn't answer, he asked his sister, who had her arm round his waist, 'Where is our father?' She looked away, and so he turned and asked his uncle, who walked behind him with a hand on his shoulder: 'Bone Hook – where is he?'

And his uncle, too, lowered his eyes. And each time his question was unanswered, Bitten-by-a-Fox was the more certain of what the answer was.

When they were all gathered into one tent, around the fire, they told him what had happened to his father, Bone Hook.

'In the summer,' said White Reindeer, 'new babies

85

were born, but when the winter came, and we changed, the babies didn't change. We were wolves, and they were still small babies. What could we do? In winter a wolf-pack must travel far, to hunt, but we could not, because we could not leave the babies. So we stayed, and the babies drank wolf's milk. But what were we to eat? What were the wolf-mothers to eat, to keep their milk? We were in the South and around us were sheep and chickens and goats – but nothing that a wolf could safely hunt! The farmers had traps and guns. We took chickens, and the farmers came after us. They set their traps, but we knew traps when we saw one! They lay in ambush for us, but we knew they were there – we could hear them, smell them. And so they hunted us on horseback, with dogs. We scattered, we ran every way, and the dogs and the horses and the men – '

Fox's sister leaned to him and took one of his hands, as his mother took his other. 'The dogs and the men and horses followed our father.'

'He ran but he was old,' said White Reindeer. 'They ran him down: he could not stand. The dogs bit him to death. They tore pieces from him.'

Bitten-by-a-Fox bowed his head into his own hands, into his mother's and his sister's hands. From behind him came a brother's arms to hold him; his brother's head rested on his back.

Said White Reindeer, 'They chopped off Bone Hook's head, and his wolf's tail, and his paws. They laughed and danced about, and waved the pieces of him in the air.' She sighed through tears, with a sound like cloth tearing. 'They did not know he was Bone Hook; they thought him a wolf.'

Fox lifted his head from their hands, and tears were

running down his face. 'They would have killed him anyway – those people – they would have killed him because he was a Lappie!'

The others did not understand, because they had not been tricked by townspeople, or called a Lappie, or dirty or stupid by people who hated them only because they were who they were. But they understood his grief, and they held him, and rubbed his back, touched his hair in sympathy, and cried with him, while Fox remembered how his father had asked him not to go away, and that his father had died without knowing whether his youngest son was alive or dead.

White Reindeer stroked Fox's hair and wiped tears from his face with one knuckle of her hand. 'The babies born that summer all died in the winter,' she said gently, so that there should be no more bad news to tell. 'We could not keep them warm, nor their mothers fed well enough to feed them.'

'It was a terrible curse that the shaman put on us,' said her sister, Little Fish, who had grown very thin and ill. 'Why did he hate us so much?'

Bitten-by-a-Fox raised his face, and the firelight shone golden over the tears on it. 'Kuzma!' he said. 'Kuzma, Kuzma! – I have found no one to help us; only people to trick us. There is no reaching Kuzma . . . But if a name gives power, if naming the White Grandfather calls him to us, then – Kuzma! Kuzma! Kuzma! I have my father's death to settle with you! Kuzma! We have these babies' deaths to settle with you!'

More people reached over to hold his hands and his arms, thinking he had gone a little mad. But Fox went on chanting. The people looked at each other. Name the bear, and the bear comes . . . Soon everyone in the tent

87

was chanting Kuzma's name, swaying in rhythm, and clapping. 'Kuzma! Kuzma! Kuzma!'

'We have our wolves' shapes to pay you for!' Bitten-by-a-Fox cried.

'Kuzma! Kuzma!'

'We have our reindeer's loss to pay you for!'

'Kuzma! Kuzma! Kuzma!'

'I want to tell you of my father's death!'

'Kuzma!'

The sound travelled through the air, disturbing the few reindeer the people had now, making a bird fly up, a hare's ears twitch. It travelled further. The name was the shaman's only and true name. Though he was far distant, perhaps a world or two away, the sound of his name reached him.

He listened, and smiled. He knew who called him. He knew why. He didn't answer. A shaman comes and goes as he pleases, and answers no call unless he wishes to answer.

5

Am I dreaming (asks the cat) when I sleep in the links of my golden chain; or am I dreaming when I think I wake and walk round and round this tree, telling my stories, singing my songs?

Ambrosi's sleep (says the cat) is no longer so deep, or so safe. Ambrosi dreams.

In winter, through the long darkness, Ambrosi and Malyuta hunted. In spring they travelled to the city and delivered their furs to the Czar's storehouses; and they spent their summers in whichever of the Czar's villages was nearest to the land they meant to hunt. It was always a different village. Never, since Ambrosi's grandparents had asked them to leave, had they summered in the same village for two years together.

The summer work, in the villages, was the harvest. Summer was short, the coming winter would be long and cold, and the grain must be gathered as soon as it was ripe, before bad weather had a chance to spoil it. Malyuta and Ambrosi helped with the harvesting, working long, long hours through the summer's long, single day, and sleeping, exhausted, while the day continued.

At one harvest, in one village, Ambrosi straightened from his work to ease his back and, while standing, he sang. His voice rose from the field in the still air, strong and clear, and if he was a little breathless, that only made the notes more beautiful.

Everyone who heard him stopped in their work. They listened as his voice moved from note to note; and they held their breaths, fearing that the next note would be untrue. But it was not, and the people kept yet more still, frozen with their tools in hand, listening . . .

> *I wish I was in a lonely valley*
> *Where no other can be found,*
> *Where the pretty small birds do change*
> *their voices*
> *So every moment, a sweeter sound.*
>
> *I wish I was far, far from here now*
> *Flying over the deepest sea*
> *Diving down the deepest ocean*
> *Where love nor care can follow me –*

The song had a slow, sad music and Ambrosi's voice lingered over the words, as if he truly longed for that lonely valley and that deep, distant sea. The song frightened Malyuta. The tune and the voice made him hold his breath, but the words were a punch above his heart. And when the song ended, he looked about and saw that all others in the field were standing still, even those he would have thought too far away to have heard. All the faces had a look of shock, as if they had been told something they had not expected. And then the people began to walk away from the field. They dropped their tools, they left the harvest unfinished, they left their friends and families and each person walked away from every other. Some lay down in the corners of the fields and hid their faces; others went alone into the woods, or shut themselves up in their houses. Every person found their own hiding place, and no more work was done that day.

And the headman of the village came to Malyuta and asked, 'Will you and your son be returning here next summer?'

'No,' said Malyuta, knowing why the man asked. 'We shall go to another village next year.'

'Good,' said the headman, who was responsible for seeing that the village work was done. 'Good.'

And Malyuta said to Ambrosi, 'Don't sing when we are with others. Keep your singing for the winter when there's just us.' He tried to make what he said kinder by adding, 'Your singing is too good for them.'

Often, in the villages, when the people were too tired to work anymore, they would draw together outside one of the houses. The older people would sit on benches or chairs brought from the house, the younger would sit or lie on the grass or in the white dust. It was always hard to go to bed in summer, when the light was still bright. They passed around food and drink, and they talked. Memories of other harvests would lead on to other memories, and soon they would be telling old tales of what grandfather did, and what grandmother said. And someone would say, 'That's like the old story of . . .' And the story-telling would begin.

But Ambrosi kept his stories to himself, and listened to the stories of the villagers.

The story-telling was often noisy. While one struggled to tell the tale, others would be calling out, 'No, that's not what happened! It was mice who were turned into horses, not rats!'

'What kind of horses would mice make?' the story-teller would demand. 'It was rats, I tell you, rats.'

Or there would be disagreement about the story to be told, some wanting one tale, others another, while the story-teller wanted to tell quite another. Some story-tellers were so forgetful that they needed to be helped through every step of the story by their listeners. And even while a story was being told by someone who could remember it, there were people who weren't listening, but were talking quietly of other things, or who were whisperingly explaining what was being said to children, or to people who hadn't heard.

Then, in one village, in one year, when the people had listened to some short tales and then fallen quiet, Ambrosi, who was sitting cross-legged on the ground, said,

'At the World's End, there is a well, and beside it grows an iron tree; and the leaves of the iron tree drop and rust in the well's red water . . .'

And on he went, and told of a girl who followed a long road that ended at the well; and of the heads that rose from the water, and what they said to her.

From the moment Ambrosi began the tale to the last word he spoke of it, no one interrupted; no one spoke. Ambrosi used the same words that everyone used, and his story – though it was never quite the story they expected – had many things in it which the people had heard before. And yet their food was left to the summer flies. Their cups were set on the ground beside them, and knocked over, and the drink spilt, without anyone noticing.

Some among the listeners leaned back and closed their eyes, the better to see the pictures his words made in their heads. Others leaned towards Ambrosi and stared at him, their whole bodies still while their forgotten hands fidgeted. Some so forgot themselves that they acted out the story, and mouthed the words the characters spoke. Even Malyuta was submerged and lost in the story.

When Ambrosi stopped speaking, there was a long silence as the people waited for his voice to go on, for there to be more . . . And then they blinked and looked about, took deep breaths and let out long sighs, and laughed, or got up and walked away to sleep.

The next night the villagers told no stories of their own, but kept looking at Ambrosi, until someone said, 'Tell us another story, Ambrusha.' And for many nights after that Ambrosi told stories.

With each tale he told, the villages fell more under the spell of his words. While some listened almost without breathing, others got to their feet and acted out the story with their whole bodies.

'And down the road the soldier walked, left, right, left, right, left, right,' Ambrosi said, and men, women and children stood around him and marched in place, or even went marching off down the village street for a little way, before they missed the words and came hurrying back.

The next day, the village children would act out the tale again, in their games. Often enough, too, they woke crying from nightmares where they had met the bears who prowled Ambrosi's stories.

Once, when the story of the night before had been a sad one, the people moved through the next day to its slow rhythm, with down-hung heads.

But Malyuta noticed that, during the hours when they

93

worked, the people began to look at Ambrosi warily, and to keep at a distance from him. Some people began to keep away from the gatherings where stories were told, and to keep their children away. The villagers, Malyuta saw, were beginning to be afraid of Ambrosi; and Malyuta knew that would bring neither him nor his son any good.

So he said to Ambrosi, 'Keep your stories for the winter, lad. Don't you see the looks you're getting?'

Ambrosi told no more stories, even when he was asked, but kept them to himself and listened to the village story-tellers in silence.

But when he was apart from other people, Malyuta often heard him singing,

> *I wish I was in some lonely valley*
> *Where no other can be found,*
> *Where the small birds do change their*
> *voices*
> *So every moment a sweeter sound . . .*

When winter came Malyuta and Ambrosi left the village and returned to the loneliness of the snow-plains. Now that Ambrosi was grown and a skilled hunter, they often worked alone, and as they returned to their camps at different times, or while the other was sleeping, they often didn't speak to each other for a long time. But when they did meet, they would lean together, often wrapped in the same blanket, and laugh. Malyuta would tell his stories of Yefrosinia, of gluttons and bears; and Ambrosi would tell his stories. Malyuta didn't mind falling under their spell. He didn't fear that his son's words would steal anything from him.

It happened one day that they went out together to

check the snares and found, in one of them, a sable. It had been caught by the neck and strangled, and it lay on the snow like a soft black bag of fur. Blood had trickled from the wound and from its nose, and had stained the snow with a darkness not so dark as the black fur.

Malyuta touched his son's head and said, as he always did when they caught sable, 'Black as sable, red as blood, white as snow.'

Ambrosi took off his skis, because he was quicker at doing that than his father, and knelt to free the body from the snare. He handed the snare to Malyuta: it would be reset shortly. Malyuta leaned on his bow and watched his son's neat, quick movements with satisfaction. Ambrosi drew his knife and Malyuta got ready to watch the skinning of the sable – but instead, Ambrosi opened his pouch and took out a strip of dried reindeer meat. He cut a piece from the meat and then pried open the sable's stiff jaws with his knife. All its sharp, dead little teeth glittered in the light of the snow and moon, and the gape of its mouth and throat made it seem even more dead than before. Ambrosi placed the piece of meat he had cut in its mouth.

Malyuta was going to ask what he was doing, but before he could, Ambrosi began to sing. His voice was a little hoarse in the cold, sharp air, but it was as clear and true on the notes as ever, and wound a net of music around the words. Each new turn left Malyuta's listening ear longing for those notes again, and every time he would have spoken, that longing silenced him.

But the song was a strange one, and made him want to ask more questions. Forgive us, said the words: we needed your fur, we needed your body. Forgive us; you

95

have killed too. Take this meat, a gift for your journey – there is the road: don't be afraid!

Each word and phrase seemed to mean more to Malyuta than the simple sense they held. With each word, each beautiful phrase of music, the song became more eerie and its music more steely cold and ringing. The cold of the world he stood in pressed closer around him, and the black sky of cold stars was clamped more tightly to the frozen earth. Malyuta shivered strongly: a bird had flown over his grave.

Malyuta knew the song. When he had been young, he had learned his trade from older hunters, and he had heard them sing snatches of the songs the shamans sang to guide the dead from this world to the Ghost World. He had never heard more than a few words, but here was Ambrosi singing a shaman song, complete and perfect. Where did you learn that song? he wanted to ask, but he wanted to listen more, and besides, he was afraid.

Ambrosi ended the song and, with his knife, began stripping the skin from the sable; but Malyuta was still held silent and couldn't ask his questions. He felt shy of his son.

When the fur was stripped, and rolled, and packed in Ambrosi's pack, they moved on over the snow, to find a new place to set the snare, and to check the others. Malyuta still kept silent and, beneath his shyness and his fear, anger began to grow. So he said, 'Why stuff a dead mouth with food? It's waste! And wasting time! Why sing to a dead sable? And why such a dreary song? If you must sing, you should sing something cheerful.'

Ambrosi looked at him, but didn't answer. He went on pushing with his bow, and gliding forward on the long ski strapped to his right foot. Pushing and sliding, pushing and sliding – 'And why go so fast?' Malyuta demanded. 'You'll wear yourself out.' He said this, not because he thought Ambrosi would tire himself, but because he was angry to see himself being left behind.

Ambrosi made a wide circle over the white snow, under the black sky, and came back to his father. As he came, he raised his head and looked at Malyuta and saw him clearly. His father was broader and heavier than he had been, and his shoulders were more humped, his head more bowed. The beard that poked from his hood and hung down the front of his coat was white with age as well as ice.

My father is old, Ambrosi thought. He might not live to see winter end this year.

Ambrosi came back to his father's side, and was careful not to outpace him again.

On their way back to their tent, they passed the circling paw-prints of a bear.

Ambrosi dreamed often now. He dreamed of a bear coming to their tent and walking around it. He dreamed of the bear coming into the tent; and sometimes the bear was a man.

He dreamed of music: the sweet, shrill call of a flute, fluttering up like a bird, drawing out its note purely, and swooping down. One night Ambrosi lay on the snow under the high black sky and listened. He heard the warm breath of the flute player vibrate in the pipe, and then the call again, achingly perfect. Ambrosi didn't want to move or open his eyes in case his movement made the music end.

When it did end, he kept still, as a hunter keeps still when he wants a nervous animal to return. He felt the lids heavy over his eyes, and the jump of his heart beating within him. Then he felt warm skins over him and under him: he heard a fire crackling as it burned, and smelt its reek, and realized that he was not lying on snow. He was in the tent.

Ambrosi opened his eyes – or did he wake? – and saw the golden light of the fire on the sloping hide walls. Beside him, sat the flute-player, cross-legged, the long painted wooden pipe across his knees. Tumbled behind the man was a thick, heavy cloak of yellow-white fur. Over the shoulders of this cloak fell the man's hair and beard, long, dark hair streaked with broad stripes of grey. The man watched Ambrosi intently. His eyes, made large by the shadows above and below them, were so dark they were almost black.

The man was no stranger. This was the bear, and the man who had come into his grandmother's house and demanded that Ambrosi should go with him. Ambrosi looked about and saw that the tent was empty except for himself and the flute-player. Malyuta, who had been sleeping beside him, wrapped in skins, was gone, and so were all the dogs. They had not even left anything behind, not even a bone or a heap of snares. So this is still a dream, Ambrosi thought.

The visitor smiled. His face, until then, had seemed gentle, but the smile showed sharp teeth. 'My true and only name is Kuzma. Now tell me your name.'

'Ambrosi.'

'The hunter named you Ambrosi, as he names his dogs. Tell me your *true* name.'

A hiccup rises in the throat before you know it. When Kuzma asked him what his true name was, it seemed to Ambrosi that he was about to hiccup out a name he had never heard before. That frightened him, and he choked it down. 'My name is Ambrosi. I have no other name.'

Kuzma's face had seemed gentle, and cruel; now it was sad. 'If you had been given to me on the day of your birth, I would have sung you from your childhood, and then I would have asked you your true name. You would never have gone by any other. But now you have forgotten it.' He raised the pipe to his lips again, and Ambrosi held his breath, eager to hear the music. Again Kuzma blew those sweet, vibrating, calling, calling notes that filled Ambrosi with pain, because as soon as they began they must end. But before the note ended, he was startled by knocks against the stiff hide of the tent walls: knocks and rustles, knocks and flappings, and furious bird-cries. There were birds outside the tent, beating their wings against it, trying to come in.

Kuzma drew another note from the flute, another call – and in a shower of cries and feathers, birds came in by the smoke-hole at the top of the tent, came spiralling down through the smoke and heat of the fire, breaking the light into shadows with their fluttering wings.

Kuzma lowered the pipe. 'The power to call,' he said. He raised the long flute, the firelight rippling along its length, and gestured to the poor birds peeping and battering themselves against the tent, slicing the smoke with their wings. One fell onto the skins that carpeted the tent, its wings hurt. 'The power to heal. The power to change, the power to blast; the power to make clear and the power to hide. You have these powers.'

'No,' Ambrosi said.

'When you told your stories,' said Kuzma, 'you called the people; your words bound them in place. They obeyed you; they lived in your words. You made them

99

dance to your tune, and they feared you. You are a shaman half-made, and you must be a shaman. A shaman knows his own true name. What is your true name?'

Again Ambrosi felt his throat move to speak without his will, but he swallowed and pushed himself further away from the shaman and the fire, just as Malyuta had once stepped back from the shaman and the blaze of midnight sun.

Kuzma nodded and smiled, holding his flute upright, like the pole of a banner. The birds captured by his music beat about his head and landed on his shoulders, but he took no notice of them. One still lay, kicking and hurt, by his knee. 'My true and only name is Kuzma. Seven times seven times I have nested in the Iron Ash in Iron Wood, sleeping in the nest of the bear, and the bear fed me. Seven times seven times I have been born, and each time one of my own kind has claimed me, and has asked me, 'What is your name?' Seven times seven times I have answered, 'Kuzma' and I have remembered that I am a shaman; each time a greater shaman with more to learn and more to teach. You are not Ambrosi. That is only the name the hunter gave you, and he is nothing. You are my apprentice. Tell me: what is your true name?'

The name rose again into Ambrosi's throat, but he felt that he was being pushed and dragged into a darkness where he could see nothing and be certain of no safety. The firelight on the tent walls dimmed; he could feel the cold from outside. 'I am Ambrosi!' he said.

Kuzma smiled. One of the many birds fluttering in the tent alighted on the end of the flute, and Kuzma reached out and put the bird on Ambrosi's head. Ambrosi ducked under the bird's tiny weight and light, scratching feet, and smiled as the bird whistled.

'Ambrosi!' Kuzma said. 'Immortal! The hunter gave you the name only. I can give you three hundred years of life, and I can teach you to climb the Iron Ash when your three hundred years are done, and sleep in your nest until the Gate opens for you again. Come with me. I shall not silence your singing. I shall teach you to do more with words than tell stories. Come with me now: remember all you knew and learn more.' The shaman held out his hand, smiling. His eyes and teeth shone in the firelight, and his face looked sharp and wicked. But then the fire flickered, and the shaman's face vanished in darkness. When the fire flared and the face reappeared, it was not wicked, but sad, and stared at Ambrosi, longing for company.

Ambrosi looked at the offered hand and trembled, shivered, because he wanted to take the hand; and he was deeply afraid.

'Do you want the valley where the birds change their voices?' asked the shaman. 'Every moment a sweeter sound. Do you want to fly over the sea? Do you want to fly under it? No love or care will follow you if you tell me your true name and come with me.'

Still Ambrosi crouched by the fire and trembled. Outside the firelight, where Kuzma would lead him, was a darkness that hid traps and falls and snares. But if he stayed safe in the firelight, then he must also stay silent when others sang and told stories. If he stayed in the firelight, he must never know his true name. His wishes were pushing and dragging him into Kuzma's dangerous darkness. He jumped to his feet, meaning to leave the tent and escape – but as soon as he rose, he woke, and was lying on the floor of the tent, with a dog sleeping across his legs and Malyuta snoring beside him.

He said nothing of his dream to Malyuta. If it was no more than a dream, then why tell of it? If it was more than a dream, then there was nothing that Malyuta could do to help him, even if, as he used to promise, he made himself a roof, a ship, a sled, a wall for Ambrosi's protection. So Malyuta went on with his work, and laughed about how much sleep the young needed, never knowing that every time Ambrosi slept, he dreamed, and that into every dream came Kuzma.

Sometimes Kuzma came into the tent where they slept. Sometimes Ambrosi was sitting in his grandmother's house, which he had not seen for years. The door would open, letting a blaze of midnight sunlight fall over the wooden floorboards – and over those floorboards would come Kuzma's bear-clawed boots. In a summer woodland, or a winter snow-plain, or in some place so strange that Ambrosi had no words for it, Kuzma would come, in his bear or man shape.

Kuzma would lift his flute to his lips and play music that made Ambrosi feel its beauty so strongly that it exhausted him, and he could not bear for it to begin. But once the music had begun, swaying and folding, coming again and again to the same lovely phrase that caught the heart on a hook, then Ambrosi could not bear for it to end . . . The music brought birds wheeling down from the sky, so spelled by the playing that they could be picked up in the hand. It brought wolves from the forest, and bears, coming ever closer, a step at a time, unable to break away and tame as pet dogs. Ambrosi saw trees take a step forward and bow down. So entranced was Ambrosi by the music that he felt his own body twist and re-form itself to the music's will, until he crept to Kuzma's feet, as a sable.

In every dream, Kuzma asked: 'What is your true name?' Ambrosi hated the question. He feared the unknown Kuzma would lead him to, and so he struggled not to know, not to hear, and never to speak, his own true name. But Kuzma's music made him feel his weariness of Malyuta's world, where no village wanted him unless he was silent, and it made him long, with a sharp curiosity, to know what his true name was. He didn't, wouldn't know his own true name; but he could never forget it.

And there was Malyuta. Once Ambrosi had looked clearly at Malyuta and had seen how old he was, he could never again look at him and see the strong father Malyuta had once been. He noticed, instead, how deaf Malyuta was; how often, and how loudly, he had to speak to him before the old man heard. Malyuta was becoming weak and slow. He could not draw his bow so often as he used, before his arms were too tired to draw it again. He felt the cold, and he coughed, and often Ambrosi had to leave him behind in the tent, with a dog to keep him company, as Malyuta had once left Ambrosi behind. Now it was Ambrosi who brewed thick, hot, buttery tea and coaxed Malyuta to drink it.

Ambrosi would stare at the old man across the fire, and remember how often Malyuta had hugged him close, to keep him warm or from sheer affection; how often Malyuta had stuffed him with food, to make sure he had eaten enough; and of how often Malyuta had lovingly and anxiously brought him presents from the city. Ambrosi remembered the drum which Malyuta had brought, and which he had spoiled. Malyuta, Ambrosi knew, was coming to the end of his life.

Ambrosi dreamed; and he sat on the snow, while the stars shone bright and hard in the black sky above, and the snow-light wavered about him. And there was Kuzma, his white-yellow bearskin falling from his shoulders, and his warm-voiced wooden flute resting across his knees.

Kuzma looked at him and said, 'You are my apprentice-born. You know all that I can teach. You know all that I can give. How can you not come with me? How can you not tell me your true name?'

Ambrosi said, 'Malyuta.'

Kuzma sat quiet. His hair and beard were ruffled by the cold wind that scudded across the snow, throwing ice crystals before it with a hiss. He said, 'When you were in this world before, Malyuta was not your father. He was not born; he was nothing. When you come into this world again, Malyuta will not be your father then, nor anything. He will be lost in Iron Wood; he will be nothing. Why do you care for Malyuta now? He is as brief and passing as a spark that leaps from the fire and dies in the dark air. You are a shaman. Leave the hunter to his dying.'

The bleak loneliness of these words struck Ambrosi through as coldly as the wind, and filled him with fear and darkness. 'Sparks are warm while they last,' he said.

'Tell me your true name.'

'Malyuta loved his son.'

'He loved himself, or he would have given you to me.'

'He is an old man, and my father.'

'You and I should have no care for fathers.'

'You never knew mother or father,' Ambrosi said, 'but

I know my father and I love him. Many times I've hurt him, never meaning any hurt, and now . . .'

'Tell me your true name.'

Ambrosi could feel the name swelling out of darkness at the back of his mind. 'My true name . . .' He looked away from Kuzma and tried to see through the very walls of the dream, into waking.

'Until you tell me your true name, until you come with me, there will be no peace for you.'

'My father is old. When he dies . . .'

Kuzma leaned towards him and his dim shadow shifted on the snow. 'There is much I must teach you and I, too, have a short time left to live. There can be no waiting for this hunter's life to trickle away in slow years. Tell me your true name.'

Ambrosi shut his eyes and put his hands to his ears, as if he could block out a sound that was in his own head.

'Your true name: hear it! It is at your centre; speak it! Your true name; say it! Your true name: tell it me!'

Each command struck on Ambrosi's ears like a drum beat; with each drum beat, the sound in his head came closer and was louder. 'Syngva!' he said. 'Syngva!'

Kuzma's teeth showed white, sharp and strong through his beard. He held out his hand. 'Syngva! Come with me now.'

Ambrosi rose to his feet, as Kuzma rose, and Ambrosi's hand lifted to take Kuzma's hand. When a shaman speaks your true name, it's hard to resist. But the moment before their hands met, Ambrosi clenched his hand into a fist and turned his face away from Kuzma's. 'No!' Ambrosi said, and wrenched himself round – and woke in the tent.

He sat up and hunched over the fire, and thought of

what might have happened if he had taken the shaman's hand . . . Would he have been pulled right out of this world, body and all? It was a thought so frightening that he shook, despite the heat of the tent; but a thought so curious and wonderful that he turned it over and over in his mind.

'Are you sickening?' Malyuta asked him, later that dark day. It seemed to Malyuta that his son moved slowly and was tired quickly, like one in the first stages of an illness. Ambrosi shook his head after a moment, as if he had only just heard. That night Malyuta made him a large bowl of tea, to hearten him, and drive away whatever sickness it was. Ambrosi drank it and lay down to sleep.

And he dreamed again. He dreamed once more that he sat with Kuzma in the cold darkness that shivered with the red, blue and green of the Northern Lights. And Kuzma said to him,

Syngva: listen. I shall tell you a story.

In the beginning the Shaman who made the world called all his creatures before him, and he gave to them all thirty years of life.

'But,' said the donkey to him, 'my life is to be spent bending my back under heavy loads. I am to be kicked and beaten to make me go fast when the load on my back makes me go slow. If that is to be my life, so be it — but thirty years is too long, Grandfather.'

The Shaman pulled his beard thoughtfully, and saw that the donkey was right. So he took eighteen years of life from the donkey, and left him only twelve. The donkey was grateful.

Next came the dog. 'Grandfather,' said the dog, 'my life is all running and biting and barking, and it is a good life. But how shall I live it for thirty years? Long before then my legs will be

106

weak and lame, my teeth will be broken and worn, my bark will be unheard. Spare me this life without life.'

So the Shaman was kind, and he took twelve years of life from the dog.

Then came the monkey, and the monkey said, 'Don't make me live thirty years, Grandfather. I am only liked when I am funny. How can I be funny for thirty years? And though it pleases people to laugh at me, it is no pleasure to me to be jeered at and called fool. Take some of these years from me.'

So the Shaman took ten years of life from the monkey.

Then came man and woman, and they said, 'Grandfather, how long are we to live?'

'Thirty years,' said the Shaman.

'Oh, Grandfather,' said man and woman, 'at the end of thirty years, we shall have come to our full strength, we shall have built ourselves a house, we shall have planted a field, and we shall have children. Are we to die then, and leave all that? Thirty years, Grandfather – it's not long enough. Give us some more years.'

The Shaman was pleased that one of his creatures wanted more of the life he had created. Gladly, he gave man and woman the eighteen years he had taken from the donkey.

'Give us more, Grandfather.'

So the Shaman gave them the twelve years he had taken from the dog.

'Give us more, Grandfather.'

The Shaman gave them the ten years he had taken from the monkey.

And so men and women live seventy years in this world. And now you see, Syngva, what human life is. For the first thirty years, men and women live as the Shaman intended men and women to live. But then they must endure the eighteen years meant for the donkey: eighteen years of hard labour, of

drudgery, of heavy loads. Then come the twelve years taken
from the dog: twelve years lived weak and lame, toothless and
aching, snapping and snarling. And, at the end, come the ten
years from the monkey: ten years chattering and gibbering to
themselves, while others point, and laugh and mock. Syngva; is
this what you choose?

'Malyuta is in his dog-years,' Ambrosi said. 'I am still
living as the Shaman intended men to live. It would be
wicked to leave him now. Even when he's an old
monkey, I shall try not to make fun of him. And when he
is dead, I shall come with you.'

'You must choose now,' Kuzma said. 'Three hundred
years of life as a shaman, and power, and rebirth. Or
thirty years of human life, followed by the years the
donkey, the dog and the monkey are too proud to
endure. Now choose, choose! Once and for all!'

'Grandfather,' Ambrosi said, 'I can make no choice
until my father dies.'

Kuzma reached out his hand, and touched Ambrosi
over his heart. From Ambrosi's shirt he drew a long,
white thread. He said, 'You think that all these years I
have been tormenting you.' Again his hand reached out
and drew from Ambrosi's shirt a long, long black thread.
'You think that if you never saw me again, in dreams or
awake, you would be at peace.' A third time Kuzma
reached out, and drew from Ambrosi's shirt a thread of
bright scarlet. 'But I have been protecting you, Syngva,
from the spirits who marked you for a shaman, and who
will not allow you to refuse.' He reached out and pushed
Ambrosi backwards, so he fell back into the snow. 'Go
and live the life you choose.'

And Ambrosi fell out of his dream and into sleep on
the floor of the tent, and from that sleep he awoke mad.

Malyuta was woken by Ambrosi crawling about the tent, rolling up skins and talking loudly to the dogs, who were whining with excitement. 'There is a sable in the tent, a sable!' Ambrosi said.

There was no sable that Malyuta could see, but Ambrosi insisted that there was: it was bleeding, he said, and dragging its blood over everything – look at the trail it had left there, look there! Malyuta could see nothing.

But the invisible sable didn't go away. When Ambrosi reached for something to eat, the sable, he said, snapped at his fingers; and so he ate little. When he went out to check his snares, the sable, he said, reached them before he did. The snares were always empty, but the foot-prints of a sable were in the snow around them. When he tried to sleep, the sable came and whispered in his ear and kept him awake.

'What does it whisper?' Malyuta asked, all amusement scared out of him.

Ambrosi shook his head. The words aren't clear, he said, but they were becoming clearer. One day, soon, he would be able to hear what the sable said.

Malyuta made up his mind then to end their hunting and go to the nearest village, where he would ask for shelter and what help could be given to his son. The Czar would have to be content with the furs they had already caught. When told what his father intended to do, Ambrosi didn't argue and helped to break camp and load the sled. He only said that the sables would follow them.

During the journey to the village, Ambrosi sometimes sat silently on the sled, and sometimes he argued loudly with something that Malyuta couldn't see, telling whatever it was to go away, to stop biting, to be quiet. He would kick and strike at it, and Malyuta listened, and watched, and despaired.

When they reached the village, the people welcomed them, as they did all travellers, especially at that cold time of the year. The headman of the village took them into his hut, which was the largest and had the most room for guests, and he and his family shared with them the warmth of their stove, their food and their drink; and all they asked in return was a little gossip. But they soon noticed that Ambrosi watched things that weren't to be seen by anyone else, and that he talked, as it seemed, to himself.

'This old hunter has brought a madman amongst us,' they said to each other, and they were uneasy.

But perhaps the people could have tolerated a madman who merely talked to things that weren't there. It was when it became clear that he spoke to things that *were* there that the people began to be truly frightened. A noise, like that made by the scrabbling feet of rats, was heard in any house where Ambrosi happened to be; and Ambrosi's eyes were seen to follow the sound. Blood-stains were found on floorboards and tables; and the wood of doors and shutters was scratched, as if by claws.

Nightly Ambrosi woke the headman's family with his nightmares. 'They are biting me to pieces!' he would shout to Malyuta, who tried to quiet him. 'They bite off my fingers and hands; they are in my head, hollowing it out – !'

In the snow outside the huts, the people found footprints: the large prints of a bear, the small prints of a sable.

Stores of food were found opened and spoiled, nibbled at by sharp teeth. In any house where Ambrosi was, the lids of pots would rattle, and cups and plates would scrape on shelves, and sometimes fall to the floor and smash. Doors would open by themselves and let in the cold winter wind. At night, bedclothes would be pulled back from sleepers by no one who could be seen.

And, because of all these things, the people began to give Ambrosi and Malyuta those long, considering looks which Malyuta recognized easily enough. He and his son would shortly be asked to go away.

But soon after that he and the headman's family woke to find that Ambrosi had gone. Ambrosi's skis, arrows and bow were gone, and so had most of the traps, though the skins had been left behind.

Tracks in the snow outside showed that Ambrosi had harnessed the reindeer to the sled, and had taken the younger dogs with him, and had gone, alone, back to the snow-lands.

The villagers were sorry for Malyuta, but glad that the madman had left them. Malyuta was welcome to stay with them for the rest of the winter, they said, and, in spring, they would help him to get his skins to the Czar's storehouse, if his son didn't come back. This was no comfort to Malyuta at all.

So now Ambrosi has gone alone into the snow-plains – alone unless you count the spirits that have followed him and annoy him constantly. And what of Kuzma? I shall tell of Kuzma next (says the cat), and of the reindeer people who are now wolf people.

Do you remember the reindeer people and how Kuzma cursed them with wolves' shapes (asks the cat)? Do you remember how they chanted his name to call him?

Now I shall tell you what came of that.

Kuzma listens to the chanting of his name that tickles always in his ear. He takes out his scrying mirror and peers into its dark surface that shifts and shimmers with light and shadows, and between the light and the shadows he sees the people he cursed with wolves' shapes. And he goes to find them.

There are not many of them left. White Reindeer is dead, and so is her sister, Little Fish. They died from hunger, and from wounds inflicted by hunters. And all those babies born human by summer and daylight died in the winter when their parents became wolves; and all those cubs born in darkness and winter died in the summer when their parents became human and could not bear to look at their four-legged, hairy children.

But Bitten-by-a-Fox still lives, and he is still quick to settle squabbles among his people; and among a people with so much to suffer, the squabbles are many. Some of the people sadly remember the sweet, soft words he used to speak.

'Why fight amongst ourselves when there are so many

strangers to hate us and hurt us?' he says. 'Why help our enemies by wounding each other? Remember the farmers who set traps for us. Remember the villagers who drive us away from their houses and won't let us drink from their wells. Remember our own reindeer people who won't have us amongst them, or share so much as old dried fish with us. Keep your anger for them, friends.'

It is unhappily true that no one welcomes Bitten-by-a-Fox's people any more, not even in summer, when they have their human shapes. Their human clothes, having been hidden through the winter, are soiled, crumpled, and often torn by animals. And there is something about the people inside the clothes that makes the villagers, the farmers, and even other reindeer people afraid. They are gaunt; the bones of their faces show fiercely. Through their torn sleeves and leggings, bone, muscle and tendon can be seen sliding under their skins. Their movements are too foxily quick, too cattishly light to set other people at ease.

And when they are wolves, all humans hate them. When the wolves bicker, Bitten-by-a-Fox ends it by laying down his ears and showing his teeth with a snarl. Then the others quickly fall silent, knowing that Bitten-by-a-Fox will nip them with his teeth if they don't.

Bitten-by-a-Fox has never stopped calling on Kuzma to come and hear their grievances against him. In the summer, he starts and leads the chanting of Kuzma's name. In the half-year of darkness, he leads the bleak howling that is like the winter giving voice; and though the people cannot form Kuzma's name with their wolves' throats, it is Kuzma they are calling for.

Kuzma heard them always. Now he came.

Bitten-by-a-Fox lay sleeping in his wolf's shape, outside the wolves' winter den, and he felt a tread on the frozen snow. At once he woke, scrambling up ready to run or fight. The shaman, Kuzma, crouched down beside him, his yellow-white bearskin cloak spreading on the snow, and the ghost drum at his back casting a humped shadow. Bitten-by-a-Fox tried to run as a wolf, and discovered that he was no longer a wolf, but a man, even though it is winter and the sky is black.

'You are dreaming,' Kuzma said. 'I have come into your dream. Why have you called me?'

There is so much anger and grief that Bitten-by-a-Fox has to tell, that now Kuzma is there, he cannot speak. There is too much to say and it cannot all be said in a word, which is all he has breath to speak.

'The spell that binds you to these changes is carved on a curse-bone,' Kuzma said, 'and that curse-bone is safe in the sable's nest, high in the Iron Ash at the centre of Iron Wood, in the Ghost World. You can never be free of the curse until the curse-bone is taken from the nest and broken by my apprentice – that is how I made the spell. But my apprentice will not come to me; he will not walk into the Ghost World.'

Now that Kuzma had come, Bitten-by-a-Fox forgot all his anger, and felt only fear and hope. 'I am sorry I threatened you,' he said. 'Forgive.'

'My forgiveness will not free you from the curse. Only my apprentice can do that. He can be made to walk the Ghost World road. Then he will be a shaman, but an untaught one, and he will have to turn to me, to learn all he will need to know. But if he is to be made to do this, you must work for me, Fox-Bitten. Work for me, and you will earn your release from the curse.'

Bitten-by-a-Fox stared at the snow and wondered what other shape Kuzma would inflict on them once the wolf-shape was removed. 'Will you keep your promise?'

'I make no promise,' Kuzma said. 'It is my apprentice who must break the curse-bone. Ask him to make promises. Perhaps he is better at keeping them than I. But without my help, you cannot speak to him, even when your human tongues come in season again. How will you know who he is? How will you find him?'

'Tell us what we must do,' Bitten-by-a-Fox said.

'I shall make another spell for your people. It will make every hair of their hides a spear of steel; it will make their hides shells of stone, their bones unbreakable. They must go to a certain village and howl in the streets. Take the sheep and calves from the byres, the hens from the henhouses, steal the meat from the stores. Bite the children, chase the wives. And when the hunter comes hunting you – hurt him!'

Bitten-by-a-Fox grinned at the thought of so punishing the house-dwelling people he hated. 'Will you truly make us safe from harm? If you do, I will bite everyone in the village!'

'Not you, Fox-Bitten,' said Kuzma. 'Your people. You must come with me and learn to be my messenger. I shall teach you the road to the Ghost World.'

Bitten-by-a-Fox stared, and felt his face turn white and stiff. Others of his people came close to him, put their arms about his shoulders. 'No,' said his sister to Kuzma. 'We have lost too many people to the Ghost World to let Fox go there alive.'

'Let him talk, Fox,' said his brother. 'It's another trick. A wolf's life is better than no life.'

But Bitten-by-a-Fox stared straight at Kuzma, who

115

stared back with his black eyes and said, 'I shall teach you only the road to the Ghost World Gate; you might learn as much by being sick. Learn this of me, Fox-Bitten, or I shall teach you nothing – not the name of my apprentice, nor where to find him.'

'Do you promise me that you'll make my people safe? – so that no trap or weapon can hurt them? Too many of them have died.'

Kuzma smiled. 'Do you believe in my promises?'

'Promise,' Fox said.

'I promise.'

'Then I will come with you, and learn the road to the Ghost World, and be your messenger.'

Kuzma began to touch the heads of the people, stroking down their hair as if he was stroking a dog's fur. As he touched them, one after another, he made a song, calling on their hairs to become steel knives, their hides to become hard as iron. And, as Kuzma touched them, Bitten-by-a-Fox saw grey hair springing from their heads between pointed ears, and more grey hair growing down their backs. They were turning back into wolves as he watched.

'When you wake, little brothers, little sisters,' Kuzma said, 'there will be a raven. Follow the raven, and it will lead you to the village you are to haunt.' Kuzma stood, his bearskin cloak falling about him. He pointed to Bitten-by-a-Fox. 'But you must follow me.'

Bitten-by-a-Fox started up, and found that he, too, had returned to his wolf's shape. Unhappily, his ears and tail low, he followed after Kuzma's bear-clawed boots, out of one dream and into another. He and Kuzma are out of this story for a while (says the cat).

Only shamans travel the road to the Ghost World more than once, and it is best left to them.

The other wolves woke from their dream of Bitten-by-a-Fox leaving them, and found him gone. Then they knew their dreams had been true visions, and looked for the raven that was to be their guide. A black bird against a black sky, it was hard to see until it swooped close to the snow. The wolves rose and stretched and, in single file, trotted over the snow, following the flight of the raven for mile after mile. And they were led to the village where Malyuta was, alone, without Ambrosi.

The village was half-lost in the snow that piled deep about its walls and drifted to the wooden roofs. Paths had been dug through the snow to byres, storehouses, bath-houses and the frozen well. The wolves sat at a distance, and they looked at the village and laughed, tongues hanging out of their mouths between sharp teeth. And then they howled, a freezing part-song, a ghost song to guide Bitten-by-a-Fox on his way to the Ghost World, and to let the villagers know that they had come.

In the following days the people of the village, making the cold journey from their warm houses to their cold stores, found the doors of the storehouses forced open, even against the drifts of snow. They found the leather hinges gnawed through and the doors clawed. Their stores of meat and fish had been knocked to the floor and trodden, chewed, carried away. And in the snow round the storehouses they found paw-prints, scores of paw-prints, trodden over one another; and grey wolf-hair caught on the wood of the door-frame. At night, they heard, resounding from the sky and hills around their winter-lost village, the triumph song of the wolves who had robbed them. The people were angry, and they were afraid.

Every night the wolves came, to feast on the stores the people had laid by to feed themselves through the winter. Even when the people stood on guard, the wolves came, half-seen grey shapes in the darkness; and the wolves sat and showed their teeth at the frightened people who waved sickles and knives. Even when a thrown axe squarely hit a wolf in the flank, it ran away with a mocking, rocking gait, grinning back over its shoulder, quite unhurt.

The wolves grew bolder. They walked in the village street and sat down outside the house doors, almost like house dogs – but no one wanted to pat them. People peeping from behind the double windows of the houses or opening the outer doors a crack would see them there, and wonder fearfully why they were waiting. The villagers began to be afraid to leave their houses. They would take axes and kitchen knives and carefully edge out through their doors, and quickly duck back when they saw the haunting wolf-shapes fade away into the half-light of darkness and snow.

The wolves came and scrabbled at the doors with their nails; and the people inside clutched at each other, and knew, with dread, that if the hinges on their doors had been leather and not iron, then these wolves would have chewed through them and come into the very house, perhaps to steal the food from the fire or, if they wanted softer meat, the baby from the cradle.

Wolves scratching at the doors, wolf faces looking in at the windows; the padding of wolf feet through the snow on the roof, and wolf growls down the chimney. And, every night, the beautiful, terrifying wolf carols about the village, songs celebrating – what? The people feared to know.

The people came together to decide what to do. From all the houses they came, along the icy paths walled on each side with snow, anxiously looking over their shoulders to make sure that the wolves weren't near. They came to the headman's hut, where Malyuta moped in a corner. The headman's house was soon stuffed to the roof with heat, and chatter, the stink of fatty candles burning and the fumes of vodka. The golden light fell over hunched shoulder, hanging plait, beard and boot and glass.

'Look at him there in the corner – old Malyuta!' said a man. 'He's a hunter, isn't he? And here we are, beset by wolves! Why doesn't he get off his backside and do something about them?'

The headman scratched his beard and his nose, and said, 'His son . . .'

'Ah, his son! Don't we all have troubles with our sons?'

'Children are sent to break our hearts, true enough,' said another.

'Hey, Malyuta – Malyuta! What are you going to do about these wolves, eh?'

Malyuta looked up from his corner. He had heard the wolves howling about the village; he had heard the complaints about stolen food, and wolves in the streets, but his mind was so full of worries and regrets that he had paid hardly any attention. Wolves do come close to villages in winter; that was all he thought.

'When are you going to trap them for us, Malyuta? We can each one of us have a wolf-skin coat!'

'Something must be done before they rob us of all our winter stores, Malyuta,' said a woman.

Malyuta nodded, feeling a little ashamed of himself for not noticing before how frightened people were. 'I will set traps.'

'Good!' said a man, and clattered his glass on the table. People began to tell Malyuta all about these wolves. They could understand human speech: they listened outside the houses and, when they heard people say that they were going out to the storehouse or byre, they lay in wait for them.

Malyuta listened and smiled. He knew wolves, and he knew how a good story grows. 'Well then,' he said. 'I shan't say how I'm going to trap them in case they're listening! I shall just do it.'

The next day he set about his work, and he found it unnerving. The task he had set himself was to make a pole trap near the robbed storehouses, to catch the wolves if they came there again. He hacked a hole in the hard ground, and stood a pole upright in it – a pole with a narrow notch cut near its pointed top. On the point, he would fix the bait. The wolves would reach up the pole, scrabbling to reach the bait, and sooner or later, one of the wolves would catch its paw in the notch, which would close about the paw and hold the wolf there until Malyuta came to kill it. Malyuta had made many of these traps in his time, but never had he made one while a circle of wolves sat at a little distance, watching attentively, and seeming to laugh. Many times Malyuta stopped work to take up his iron-shod staff and drive them away. They would scatter and run a little distance, but they would soon return. The villagers had spoken more truthfully than he had thought: these were not ordinary wolves.

He set snares too, at places where the paw-prints showed the wolves often walked. And he went back to the warmth of the headman's hut feeling better for, if the wolves were unusually bold – well, they would end in the traps the sooner.

But the traps didn't catch a single wolf, though all the baits were taken. And still the wolves walked in the streets and their whiskered faces peered in at windows. The clicking of their claws was heard on roof-tops, and they sang their carols from the roof ridges as they might from a hillside. So Malyuta went out on his skis to set more snares and iron traps about the countryside, thinking that perhaps the wolves were more wary close to the houses than they would be elsewhere. To his own unease and dismay, he was followed by a trail of wolves who watched him set the traps. And, when he checked the traps, the wolves watched him discover that all the baits had been taken without a single trap catching so much as a grey hair.

He made up his mind, as he rested in the headman's hut, that he would have to go out after the wolves on skis, with his iron-sheathed staff and his knife.

'Aren't you afraid to go out there after them, all alone?' the headman's daughter asked him.

'A man's a fool who isn't afraid of the wolf he's trying to kill,' Malyuta said. 'But a wolf will always run from a man if it can, and it won't turn to fight until it's past all else. The man will always win if he keeps his head. The wolf can bite, and it can bite hard, and a wolf-bite always goes bad – but a wolf is not a bear. Yes, I'm afraid, sweetheart, but no more than it's wise to be.'

But he told less than the truth. He was very afraid. He had often hunted wolf on skis, alone – but now he was old, and he had never hunted wolves that followed him and watched what he was doing. He felt a tightness about his heart, a foreboding that, if he hunted these wolves, it would be his last hunt. And his greatest dread was that he would never see his son, his Ambrosi, again. But what could he do? He was a hunter, and the people had asked for his help. To refuse it after they had sheltered him would be ungrateful.

When he left the village, carrying his skis and staff, there were no wolves waiting in the streets, and he thought this strange. He walked through the tunnels the villagers had dug through the deep snow, and left the few houses of the village behind. He stopped and put on his skis, the longer one on his right foot and, with a shove from his iron-sheathed staff, he slid over the snow and the village soon dropped into the darkness and silence behind him.

Then he saw the wolves. They slunk out of the darkness and looked at him with yellow eyes, or eyes white as ice, and then they faded into the dusk.

Malyuta was an old man, but he could still make a day's journey of forty miles on his skis. And so the wolves led him, ten, twenty, thirty miles from the village. Close around him it seemed that the snow sparkled with ice and gave light; but only a short distance ahead this snow-light mixed with darkness to a deep twilight, and a little further, and then a little further ahead, was deeper and deeper darkness. So as Malyuta skimmed over the snow, further and further from the village, the darkness closed behind him and wrapped him in silence.

There, in that snow-lit hush, the wolves stopped running from him. Keeping the silence of the hunting wolf-pack they turned back, running quickly through the shimmering dark, running to be behind him, to be at both sides of him, to be in front of him. Malyuta came to a halt on his skis. Many times he had seen wolves hunt, but never before had he been the creature they hunted; and the sinister, creeping lope with which they came towards him made him quail like any timid little reindeer calf.

He drew his knife and he gripped his staff more tightly, ready to strike the blow that would break the back of the first wolf to attack him. He had never before known a wolf that would not run from a man, but he knew that these wolves were not going to run any more.

One wolf ran quickly towards him, then jumped lightly aside when it saw he was ready for its attack – but another wolf ran in from another side. He could see their cold blue eyes, fringed by fur hung with ice crystals just as his beard was hung; he saw their white teeth gleam against their black lips. Malyuta turned and twisted as quickly as he was able, threatening one wolf with his knife, fending off another with his staff. He wished he had time enough to get off his skis, for though they had helped him glide swiftly across the snow, now it had come to this close fight, they hindered him. But there were many wolves, and they were lithe and fast. While Malyuta struck at one with his staff, another ran in and drove its teeth deep into Malyuta's thigh, above his boot – drove in its teeth and tugged, with all the strength of its back and shoulders to pull Malyuta down as a wolf pulls down a reindeer.

Malyuta yelled with pain and fear as his flesh was

123

parted by the wolf's teeth, and he struck hard again and again at the wolf that held him. The wolf didn't feel the blows or release its hold.

And now three more wolves ran in, biting him where they could. Two as quickly released their holds, but one of the wolves got its teeth into the arm that held the staff, and was joined by another wolf. Their teeth set fast in the wolf's unbreakable biting hold, they dragged down the arm, dragged Malyuta down to the snow. The white turned red.

Malyuta had his knife in his hand and, with it, he struck at the wolves, but couldn't hurt them. The knife blade broke. Malyuta yelled aloud – the only sound in all that great space and silence, for the wolves made no sound. A big young wolf loosed its hold on his leg and seized his knife arm. Another wolf clambered onto his chest with heavy, stamping paws, to reach his unprotected throat. The wolves crowded close, and bit and harried Malyuta and dragged him about on the bloodied snow like a helpless calf.

Then the wolves let loose their holds and scattered away from Malyuta's body, and crouched at a little distance. For over the snow, at a fast run, was coming a bear, a white northern bear, which stood erect and became Kuzma. With his bearskin cloak hanging and folding heavily about him, he strode over the snow, and crouched beside Malyuta, who still choked and stirred on the snow. The wolves, watching, licked bloodied muzzles and paws.

Kuzma looked at the snow, bright scarlet near Malyuta, fading pink as it soaked through the ice crystals. He looked at the whiteness stretching away into the glimmering darkness. He looked up at the intense blackness of the sky, and the intense glittering of the white, uncaring stars. 'Black, and white, and red, Malyuta,' he said.

For Malyuta, all was fading to darkness as his blood continued to pour out on the snow, as so many sables, and foxes, and wolves caught in his traps had poured out their blood. But he recognized Kuzma's voice. He tried to speak, but couldn't; and instead tried to reach out for Kuzma's hand.

Kuzma would not take his hand, but picked up snow and dropped the snow into Malyuta's gaping mouth, filling and blocking the mouth so that Malyuta's spirit could not escape with his last breath. Squatting beside the body, Kuzma began to sing, weaving a net of words about the head, fastening the words to Malyuta's hair and flesh, imprisoning his spirit. When the spell was made and fixed, Kuzma picked up Malyuta's fallen knife from the snow. It was a large, heavy knife. Kuzma wrapped his fingers in Malyuta's hair and, with one, two, three blows of the heavy knife, he hacked through Malyuta's neck and lifted the head free. The wolves scattered at the noise.

Kuzma raised his head and made a calling, clicking noise with his tongue. From beyond the circle of wolves another wolf came trotting, a young, thick-coated Arctic-grey wolf. It went up to Kuzma and looked at him with ice-blue eyes. Kuzma dropped the head into the snow and said, 'Take it.' He watched as the wolf lifted the head in its mouth, by the hair. 'Now,' said Kuzma, 'I shall tell you how to find my apprentice.'

7

Do you remember (asks the cat) how Ambrosi went alone into the snow-lands?

He is so lost that only a shaman could know where to find him.

The blackness of the silver-sparked sky glared down on the snow, and the snow's frozen surface glittered with an intricate pattern of frost stars. The air prickled with the snapping of ice crystals which was silence. In every direction, endlessly, the black sky and the white snow stretched away. Here, in this freezing, silent wilderness Ambrosi lived with his shaggy blue-eyed dogs.

He took no furs. If the snares he sometimes remembered to set caught a sable or a fox, then he ate it. Or he shot a bird or took a fish from below the ice of a frozen river, always giving thanks to the animal's spirit, and replacing its bone in the water or the land.

He could not hunt easily, for the bear and the sable followed him everywhere, in and out of sleep. A sable chittered in his ear, calling to him, commanding him, claiming him. The bear would follow him over miles of frozen snow, in darkness, where no help was to be found. When he ran, the bear ran and caught him. And then the bear ripped him with its claws and opened him up, bit his head, and his arms, and his legs from his body, and would say, with a man's voice, 'When you are put back together, you will be a shaman.'

Ambrosi would blink, and find his head on his shoulders, his arms and legs in their proper places. 'A dream,' he would think, 'a nightmare.' And then he would find the scars around his fingers, around his wrists and ankles, around his elbows, where he had been sewn together.

If he reached for a tool, it moved from his hand, or would turn to a sable which bit him. His dogs glared at him, and spoke and said, 'You are in the wrong place!' Strange walking shapes formed out of the darkness and snow-light, and they leaned near and whispered about him, but what they said he couldn't tell. Their breath was a wind from an ice-floe.

He was thin from eating so little, and he was sleepless and always cold. He lay in his tent, with his dogs, in darkness, and he heard the tent-flap open. He thought it was Malyuta, and whispered to him: he thought it was the bear and was silent. Sables were always with him, biting and chittering. He knew it wasn't them.

But when the fire burned, and the oil lamps lit themselves, he saw that it was neither Malyuta nor the bear. It was a wolf, a young male wolf, grey and shaggy, with ice-blue eyes. The wolf carried something in its mouth, something that was heavy for it, and that it had to straddle, and which banged against its legs. It dropped the thing onto the reindeer hides, and it rolled towards Ambrosi. It was a head, covered with a thick tangle of curling, yellow-grey hair. Ambrosi put out a hand and rolled the head over. The face looked up at him, its mouth snarling about a blockage of ice.

He looked for a long time at the face that lay tilted under his hand. He knew the face, but asked himself, why should he know a face so comically, so horribly detached from its body and free to roll about the floor? And yet he did know the old face, square and shaggy with hair and beard, like the square face of an old terrier. It took a long time for him to see that it was his father's head, Malyuta's head.

Then he lifted the head up between his hands and said, 'Malyuta . . . I left you alone when I should have been a wall to guard you, a fire to warm you . . . as you always were to me. What can I do now? What can I do?'

The wolf was hanging its mouth open, and a long red tongue dangled out. It licked the tongue round its black lips and white teeth, and then spoke in a man's voice, just as the dogs had spoken.

'I bring the head from Kuzma,' the wolf said.

Ambrosi turned his head and looked at the wolf.

The wolf rose, came closer and poked its long nose at the head in Ambrosi's hands. 'Kuzma tells me to say that your father is dead, but not gone. Kuzma caught his spirit in a net of spells and bound it to the head. I must tell you, Kuzma says, that your father will never reach the Ghost World until you take him there.'

A slight, wavering movement made Ambrosi look aside then – and he sat up with a start when he saw his father, Malyuta, sitting on the other side of the fire. Malyuta's face was as white and frozen as the snow outside the tent. His lips were stretched back over his teeth, and the outline of his teeth showed through his lips. His eyes stared at Ambrosi but there was no light or knowledge in them; and his whole shape flickered and faded with the light of the fire. The dogs and the wolf all shrank back from this awful figure, and Ambrosi felt his own hair move in the cold breeze that moved up his back and neck.

With his eyes fixed on his father's apparition, Ambrosi said, 'I won't go to the Ghost World. What then?'

'Then,' said the wolf, 'your father will be lost. Dead in this world, and with no place in any other. All that he was: lost. All the love he had for you; gone and lost. All the care he took for you; gone and lost. His voice, his words, his laughter, his fear, everything that he was: all gone, all lost. Without shelter in this world, his spirit will be blown and worn and torn by the winds.'

As if the wolf felt the power of its own words, and understood them, it lifted up its head and howled. The dogs remembered their wolfish ancestors, and whined and howled too. That sound, always so lonely, heard so close, was too much to bear. It made Ambrosi shake, and tears came from his eyes as he stared at the wavering spirit of his father.

'I don't know the way to the Ghost World,' he said.

'I know the way,' said the wolf.

Ambrosi lifted up the head by its thick, grey hair, and it hung heavily from his hand. He took water that he had melted from snow, and he carefully washed the blood and dirt from it. With his fingers he combed out the hair and beard. All the time he worked, his tears ran down his face and fell onto the head and, from across the fire, the fading spirit of Malyuta glared and grinned.

'I must go to the Ghost World, then,' Ambrosi said. 'Kuzma has won.'

'I will be your guide if you will pay the price,' said the wolf.

Ambrosi looked at it. 'What price is that?'

'In the Ghost World is Iron Wood. In Iron Wood is the Iron Ash. In Iron Ash is a sable's nest and in that nest lies a bone, a curse-bone. If I take you to the Ghost World, will you find that bone for me, and break it?'

'Anything,' Ambrosi said. 'If you will guide me to my father's peace.'

'Then come,' said the wolf, and it rose and moved towards the tent flap.

Ambrosi took up his father's head by its hair, and followed the wolf out into the darkness and the cold, without putting on his outer clothes. The cold clenched about him like biting teeth.

The wolf led him with quick brisk steps over the snow to the road: the road that leads from all worlds, whoever's dream they are, to the Ghost World, which is no dream at all.

8

The road to the Ghost World is spoken of as if there was only one road (says the cat). But there are many roads that lead there. Each of us must travel one of them once: a shaman may take a different road each time the journey is made. The road is like any road that may be seen in a dream: it may be the steepest and most rocky of mountain paths, beset with thorns and loud with falling streams, or it may lose itself in forest, or cross wide, pleasant mountains.

In a moment I may tell of the journey (says the cat). I may say: so Ambrosi and the wolf walked the road to the Ghost World and came, at last, before the Ghost World's Gate. But to make that journey is to walk in time and out of time: it takes longer than any tale I can tell – and less time than to draw a breath.

Without skis, Ambrosi walked over the snow, and under the stars, and was passed by the wind, the breath of all those who had walked the road before him. In his hand, Malyuta's head swung with closed eyes; in front of him the big grey wolf trotted. Behind him came the slow figure of Malyuta, silent, its face fixed and glaring. Ambrosi did not turn to look at it. The ghost was little like the father he remembered.

The snow beneath his feet narrowed and narrowed to

a small point of land, while the darkness grew larger and the stars shone below as well as above. From that one narrow point of land a bridge sprang and arched through the sky, a bridge faintly coloured, like the Northern Lights, in icy blue, and green and the pale red of dawn. Through the very fabric of the bridge, and its colours, the stars gleamed.

The wolf ran onto the bridge, and the bridge cried out at the light touch of its feet. The wolf turned, waiting for Ambrosi. But Ambrosi stopped and knelt, the better to examine the bridge. He looked through its shimmering colours, stretched like gauze over the darkness, and down into black emptiness filled with galaxies of stars, a darkness so deep and endless that it spelled him into stillness and calm.

The wolf whined, but Ambrosi was held by the glitter of eternity.

The wolf came back to him and said, in its man's voice, 'We have far to go.'

'I cannot cross this bridge.'

'I cross it.'

'You are one of Kuzma's creatures.'

The wolf looked behind Ambrosi and said, 'There is no turning back on this road.'

Ambrosi looked behind. Stars glittered. The land he had walked over to reach this spot had vanished, fallen away, perhaps, into the darkness between the stars that the bridge spanned.

'Look at your father,' said the wolf. 'He shivers in the wind that blows from the stars. If he does not reach the Ghost World, he will vanish into this emptiness as smoke vanishes in air.'

Ambrosi did not look back at the ghost behind him,

but he rose and stepped out onto the bridge. It swayed beneath him, but then drew tight and held – and it began to thrum, as a cable drawn tight thrums in the wind. A single, thrumming note rose about him and, as he stood on the bridge, looking down through coil after coil of brilliant stars, and infinite depths of darkness, he almost became spelled again, by the sight and the sound – but he shook his head and climbed after the wolf, that looked back at him and whined.

As Ambrosi trod over the bridge, its note changed, rising and falling. He could feel its rising curve beneath his feet, and, at the height of the arch, he saw the shape of a great and beautiful tree, winter-bare of leaves. It rose out of the empty dark with the pale, pale sheen of steel by moonlight, faintly outlined against the blackness and the stars. The stars shone through its branches, like brilliant, unseasonable fruit. He stood still, and the changing, thrumming note of the bridge steadied, but other sounds, distant and eerie, crept to his ears. The stars, every one of the thousands of stars, as it spun in darkness, was spinning its own crystalline, icy, piercing note that mingled with the thrumming of the bridge, and wove and interwove with the note of every other star. Cold, thrilling, calling harmony: poignant discord: the music of the spheres. Ambrosi stood still and silent for a timeless time, listening, hearing at every moment a new choiring, impossible to leave. This, he thought, is where the shamans learn their music, that everything must obey. He would have stayed there for ever had not the wolf come back and, gripping the hem of his coat in its teeth, tugged him on. Slowly, with heavy footsteps that made the bridge ring and hum through the singing of the stars, Ambrosi followed the wolf.

The slope of the bridge began to descend, and a wind began to ruffle the wolf's fur and lift Ambrosi's hair; and with the sound of the wind came another sound: the swinging boom and echo of a sea in a cave. Soon the singing of the stars was muffled and lost in this sea-sound, which grew louder, soothing and alarming at the same time – for who knew what the soothing might betray them to? And on the wind came a smell, a smell that both wolf and Ambrosi knew well: the smell of blood.

Beneath the last span of the bridge rushed a river, bringing an echo from the black and glittering sky about them. The river foamed; it roared as it rushed along, and it smelt of blood. It was a river of blood, tossing bones as it ran: the bones clicked and clattered together.

The bridge brought them over the chasm, over the river, into a land of darkness. Three roads led away from the bridge, but each disappeared, within a few feet, into a darkness unlit even by snow-light. Ambrosi stood mystified, not knowing which way to go, but the wolf, though its fur bristled, started for the narrowest path. Ambrosi clenched his free hand into the thick fur of the wolf's ruff, afraid that he would lose his guide in the darkness.

The darkness filled them both with alarm that the next step might take them into another such bottomless chasm as they had crossed on the bridge; or into a hard rock face, or a river, or some danger . . . In all the time they wandered in the darkness – and it might have been any time – Ambrosi felt nothing but the unseen ground beneath his feet, his father's hair in his one hand, and the wolf's fur in the other. But the air carried a stink of burning, and a sharp, sour stink of ash.

When Ambrosi had forgotten what light and seeing were like, then the darkness ahead began to be smeared with red, which quickly turned to the leaping light of fires. They went forward the quicker, and Ambrosi began to see, faintly, the wolf's fur as well as feel it. The stench of burning grew stronger, and flakes of ash began to fall and fly around them, as he remembered snow-flakes flying. And gathered round the fires, as they came nearer, they saw what had been people. Some looked like people still, and even stared at Ambrosi and the wolf as they went by. Others blew like smoke from fire to fire and looked at nothing, nor cared where they blew.

And beyond the fires was the Gate. It rose above their heads: a solid gate of dark wood, bound with iron banding, and with hinges on all sides, for this Gate opens many different ways. It was set in no wall, unless the darkness on each side was a wall. And yet it could not be walked round: the Ghost World must be entered through the Gate or not at all. One narrow path led to it, and on either side of that path was chasm.

The nearer he approached to that Gate, the more slowly Ambrosi moved, until he came to a halt. He was alive, not dead, and the Gate might not open to him. Nor did he have any wish to see what was on its other side. His father's head hung heavy from his hand.

Beneath his other hand, the wolf had begun to shudder and tremble with fear. It crouched low to the ground, its ears back. 'I have brought you here,' it said, 'but I dare not enter. The Gate opens and closes only once for those of us who are not shamans. I will wait for you, to guide you on the road back.' Then it twisted its head round to lick Ambrosi's hand. 'Remember the curse-bone.'

Ambrosi stood silently before the closed Gate. It would not open for him because he was alive, and he had not been taught the shaman's way of opening it. And though he wished to bring his father's ghost safely to its proper place, he did not want the Gate to open. His heart beat fast and distantly inside him, his breath wavered and his face chilled as he thought of the Gate closing behind him, shutting him into the world of the dead and the unborn, where he might be lost for ever. There, before the closed Gate, so far from all the living worlds, unable to go forward or back, he knew all of loneliness. But then Malyuta's ghost drifted forward from behind him, and the Gate opened. Ambrosi quickly followed behind his father's ghost, before the Gate swung shut.

Beyond the Gate was twilight, barred with the dark shadows of trees. A thin, fading path led into the trees of Iron Wood. Many people were gathered about this path, some sitting, some standing. Some looked into the darkness of the trees, which they dared not enter; others stared back at the closed Gate which would not open for them. Malyuta stopped among them, and Ambrosi stopped too, alive among the ghosts.

From the wood there came blowing the scent of burning, and the sea-scents of rosemary and thyme – and a singing. Sweet high voices rising over the swaying of deep-chested notes. Who was singing Ambrosi could not guess – it was too blank and unknowing a sound to be human, yet it was not like any bird he had ever known. It was warmer and softer than the music of the bridge and stars, and he wanted to stay and listen, not because of its strangeness, but because it sang his heart down into peace.

But then Malyuta who, in his life, had been a hunter, used to wild and lonely places, went forward along the fading path, and Ambrosi followed him. They ducked beneath the iron branches and into Iron Wood.

That was a strange, strange place. Every trunk was of smooth, cold iron, grooved like engraved iron or dusted with a rough, peeling bark of iron. Every leaf that hung on every twig was of iron, and the fallen leaves through which they trod were of iron and rust, and rattled and scraped with a heavy, iron sound. A falling leaf, in that wood, rang like a cymbal!

That wood smelt of iron and rust: the streams were red with rust. A grass blade in our world is sharp; in Iron Wood the grass had the edges of sharpened knives. The briars had thorns of steel. And yet, on these iron trees, these steel briars, were flowers so delicate that, even if they were of metal, it was of metal as fine and tender as silk, and fruit that was soft enough to bite. Malyuta, as he drifted through the trees, reached out a hand and pulled iron berries from the steel briars, and ate them. But this world was Malyuta's home now. Ambrosi, as the shadows of Iron Wood fell across him, remembered those shadows from dreams; he remembered the voice of the bear, Kuzma's voice, and he knew that if he wished to leave the Ghost World in Ambrosi's body, he must not eat its iron fruit or drink from its rusty streams.

All around them, as they wandered, the singing went on, dropping to low, low notes, until higher and sweeter voices rose over those low notes, in the most beautiful of music. Through the branches of the iron trees dipped and darted birds that glinted gold, silver and copper; and perhaps they were the singers.

Ambrosi was no longer following his father. Malyuta

137

had gone, vanished into the darkness among the trees, lost in the singing. Ambrosi was quite alone, lost in a wood, in a world where he did not belong. But Malyuta belonged here; and here all he had been, all his thoughts, all that his living head had held, would be safe. Perhaps he would lie down to sleep at the foot of a silvery iron birch, and his dreaming would add to the worlds on the other side of the Gate.

Ambrosi wandered on, timelessly, listening to the singing that filled the wood and came – in a moment or an eternity – to the very centre of Iron Wood, where the Iron Ash towered into the darkness overhead. At the foot of the Ash was a pool, its black water reflecting the steel grass blades that grew about it. Beside this pool, Ambrosi set down his father's head.

Then he looked up into the iron branches of the Ash above him, as they faded, moon-grey, into the greater darkness. He set his foot against the iron trunk, reached for a branch above him, and began to climb.

Easy to tell of his climbing; not so easy to climb so far or so long! The branches were cold and hard beneath his feet, and chilled his fingers. There showered down on him a rain of rust, scratching and rasping as it struck among iron leaves and iron twigs. He climbed and climbed until his arms would no longer lift him and his legs no longer take his weight – for in the Ghost World, as in dreams, our spirit-bodies seem as real to us as our fleshly bodies do. He rested, sitting on an iron branch with his back against the hard trunk, and listened to the music that never ceased. He watched the gold and coppery birds land on the iron twigs, shaking loose rust and iron ash-keys; and he watched the other animals that lived in the tree. A squirrel passed him many times, now running up the trunk, now down. On one large, broad iron branch there lived a herd of deer, does and fawns, led by a fine stag whose antlers mingled with the iron branches about him. On other branches there were goats and pigs, and wolves and lynx and bears. No wonder this – the Iron Ash is the largest of trees, the pivot of the worlds. All the worlds that we know and dream are clouds caught in its iron branches.

There were nests in the tree too. As Ambrosi climbed on he passed more and more. Some were neat and round, others sprawling and untidy, each according to the habit of the birds or animals who built them. And in each nest there lay an Unborn. Ambrosi peered over the edge of one nest and saw a small, naked girl child who lifted to him the oldest face he had ever seen, older than his father's, older than his grandmother's. The bottom of the nest was filled with pebbles, feathers and bones, and the little girl played with them. To Ambrosi she said, 'You have far to climb, Syngva!'

Ambrosi was alarmed at her knowing his true name – the hearing of which seemed to add another chord to the music all around him – and he turned away and climbed again.

Near the nests there were always animals, and many times he saw a squirrel pelt nuts into a nest, or a bird fly to another, carrying food in its bill. And many times, as he rested, the animals came to him, bringing him the fruits of Iron Wood. But though he was hungry, and thirsty, he knew that to feed his spirit-body on the food of the Ghost World would be to lock the Ghost World Gate against him. And though it grew harder and harder to do, he always turned away from the animals and climbed again.

He had climbed, in the Iron Ash, far above the other trees of Iron Wood. He looked down on tree-tops of grey and black iron leaves, and rust red. And around him, stars glowed in the dim Ghost World sky, as they glow in the early evening in our world. Higher still he climbed, into the thinner branches of that great Ash. The air was chill, and the peaceful music of Iron Wood faded and he heard again the chiller music of the stars. Higher still, and higher still, until even the branches of so huge an ash became thin: and there, so high, he found an empty nest. It was untidy, little more than a gathering of bedding, and it was guarded by a sable so black, it was nothing more than a shadow within the shadows of the Ghost World, until it showed its white teeth.

Ambrosi crawled along the branch to the nest. He sat astride the iron branch and looked down, through spiral after spiral of iron branches that faded, through all the greys of pearl and moon into the darkness of the forest floor. He saw the other nests that he had passed on his climb, and the faint glimmerings of the little naked creatures that lay in them, waiting for a shaman birth. He looked around him at the white stars glowing through the spreading branches of the Ash – and he knew that this was the nest he had lain in himself, with the sables to bring him food, as he listened to the music of the Ghost World and the fainter singing of the stars.

Inside the sable nest lay a scarlet flower and a flat, wide, white bone. Ambrosi picked up the bone, and saw the shaman symbols cut into it, spelling out the curse. He turned it round and round in his hands. The symbols meant nothing to him, and he could not understand the curse – but the wolf had asked him to destroy it. The bone was dry and brittle, and he snapped it between his hands, breaking the lines of symbols; and he threw it from the tree. The pieces clacked against iron branches, whirled in darkness, and fell and fell and disappeared.

There was a flurry of air, sound and wings, and a raven lighted on the nest's edge. 'White as snow, red as blood, black as sable!' said the raven, in Kuzma's voice. 'Now you are a shaman, Syngva! Now you must come to me and learn all that you once knew and all that I have learned!'

Ambrosi struck out at the raven, which lifted itself with its wings to the other side of the nest, and cawed harshly with laughter. 'You killed Malyuta,' Ambrosi said.

'He would soon have died without my help,' said the raven. 'You shall live three hundred years if you will learn from me how to work with the spirits.'

Ambrosi said, 'Three hundred years is a long time to live alone.'

The raven turned its head sideways, looked at him with one eye, and laughed its hard laugh. 'Without my teaching you will live alone and not alone.'

Ambrosi would not ask what it meant.

'The spirits will never leave you again,' said the raven. 'You belong to the sables. See, they are here now.'

And it was true, that two black sables had crept near and were looking at Ambrosi with bright, dark eyes. One carried in its mouth a small apple, a Ghost World fruit.

'They will be forever whispering in your dreams, in your waking ear; forever following you. They will call the other spirits: the wolves, the bear, the birds. They will lead you into other worlds, and you will never know which world you walk in. And do you think that the people, whose company you long for, will tolerate you? When your words raise winds, when your music makes them dance against their will? When your spirits move among them and terrify them? No, Syngva; they will send you away, as they have sent you before. You will be alone, and never alone.'

Ambrosi's head dropped: he knew that it was true. 'I don't wish to be taught what you would teach,' he said. 'I shall never be taught the shaman arts by you.' And he took the Ghost World apple from the sable, and bit into it. Its crab-apple bitterness filled and dried his mouth, but he chewed and swallowed it.

The raven stretched its neck and its long, heavy black beak towards him. 'Do you know what you have done?'

'I know what I do,' Ambrosi said.

'Now you cannot leave the Ghost World until the spirits choose you again; and perhaps they never will.'

Ambrosi bit at the apple again.

'Even as the hunter's son, even as the Czar's slave, you could live longer than this,' said the raven.

'You have made me choose,' Ambrosi said, 'between learning what you would teach and living a short life. Well, I choose the short life.'

'Do you give up three hundred years of life only to thwart me?' asked the raven.

'My life was short, but sweet to me,' Ambrosi said. 'I have seen and heard much that few others see or hear. I have been a great story-teller. Enough.'

And Ambrosi laid himself down in the sable nest, and put his hands under his face. Then he rolled lazily and said, with a smile and half-closed eyes, 'Only change is everlasting, Grandfather. I choose everlasting change.'

And then Ambrosi slept, high in the thin branches of

the Iron Ash, where the songs of the Ghost World birds rose faintly from below, and the steely choiring of the stars could be heard all around. And the sable spirits chased off the raven, and stood guard over him.

Malyuta has gone into the shadows of Iron Wood (says the cat). Perhaps he has found his way to Balder's Home, that silent palace; but whether he has or has not, we waste our concern on him now. He has gone beyond our knowledge, and he cares nothing for us anymore.

Ambrosi, too, has found his safe place; more safe than any of us can be. High in the branches of the Iron Ash, at the centre of Iron Wood, in the Ghost World, watched over by his guardian spirits: neither love nor care can follow him there.

But what of Kuzma (asks the cat)? And what of Bitten-by-a-Fox, who was left waiting on the other side of the Ghost World Gate?

I shall tell of them next.

9

Do you remember Bitten-by-a-Fox (asks the cat)? Do you remember how, being neither dead nor shaman, he remained outside the Ghost World Gate, waiting for Ambrosi to return?

Well, there he sat, whining, outside the closed Gate. When you wait, time stretches out. Even a few short minutes seems an intolerable age. Imagine, then, waiting where there is no time; where a second and a century pass at the same rate.

As the wolf waited, he saw the Gate open many times. Most who came travelled alone. The Gate opened for men and women, both young and old; for children, for babies. It opened for armies of soldiers, and shiploads of sailors, and for small parties who arrived at the Gate with the smell of burning about them, or the stink of plague hospitals. But the Gate never opened to let Ambrosi – or anyone else – out of the Ghost World.

The wolf knew when Ambrosi found the curse-bone and broke it, because the wolf-shape fell from him. His hind legs lengthened and straightened; his paws turned to hands, and when he put his hands to his face, it was human. But still Ambrosi did not come, and still Bitten-by-a-Fox waited outside the Gate.

Then he heard the air vibrate to a raven's cry and,

looking up, he saw the raven's deeper darkness in the Ghost World twilight, as it flew high over the Gate. And when the raven had flown, Bitten-by-a-Fox turned and began to walk back along the way he had come. He went slowly, and sadly, feeling that he had betrayed a friend.

When he reached the bridge, he sat down by the river of blood and wept, from loneliness and fear; a fear and loneliness made greater by the stink of the blood, and the piercing singing of the stars in the darkness. He had crossed the bridge in his wolf's shape, as Kuzma's creature; but to cross it in his own shape seemed too hard a thing to do.

But he had bright memories of his own world and his own people, and behind him lay only the closed gate to the Ghost World and – after a second or a century – he forced himself to cross the bridge, crawling on hands and knees, while the bridge thrummed.

And then the path made its way through land that was more and more like his own world, by summer and by winter, until, in winter darkness, he came to a small camp of reindeer people. The patched tents were of reindeer hide, but there were only a few reindeer, and those few were tethered near the tents. Under a black and silver sky, Bitten-by-a-Fox made his way over frozen snow, past dogs who crouched and shivered as he came near; and he entered a tent, and he lay down and slept.

He woke, in his own body, in a warm tent crowded with his own people, those few of them who were still alive. Their faces were so thin that the bone stared through the skin in an ugly way, and their hair hung lank and coarse, but they were men and women, not wolves. The curse had been broken. Silently, but with a thankfulness so great he thought he could hear it echo back from the sky, Bitten-by-a-Fox embraced them all, one after another, and they him.

Then they listened to his tale. He told of the journey to the Ghost World, of the bridge and the singing stars, of the great, cold tree, with the worlds in its branches, of the river of blood, of the darkness and the Gate.

He told of the half-shaman who had gone through the Gate, who had climbed the tree and broken the curse-bone, giving them back their own shapes – but who had not returned.

He told of his own journey back to them, of his fears and despair, and his joy now he saw them again.

'Now our troubles are over,' Bitten-by-a-Fox said. 'Now we can live as we once did, when my mother and father were alive, and we were happy.'

But there were so few of the reindeer people left, and they owned so little. They would have starved if they had tried to live as they once did. And so the last of the people parted from each other. They went to other tribes and begged to be taken in and, now that the curse was broken, they were.

In their new families, they did not speak of the time they had spent as wolves: of their howling in the village streets, and hunting down Malyuta. Such tales would not have made them welcome, and they did not want to remember. So the name of the half-shaman who freed them from the curse was forgotten; and the name of the man who led the half-shaman along the road to the Ghost World was forgotten – even the name of the shaman who sang the curse was forgotten. This is a story you will only hear from cats. Only change is everlasting.

And what do the cats know of Kuzma (asks the cat)? This: that Kuzma returned to the far North and, winter by winter, darkness by darkness of his long life, he tended the ice-apples with no one to teach of their care. Cheated and lonely, hating company and laughter, as full of spite as the sea is full of salt-water . . . Even in summer Kuzma had Loki's heart in his breast, Loki's breath in his mouth.

And did the spirits choose Ambrosi to be reborn as a shaman? And did they choose him soon or late? The cats did not (says the cat), and that is all I can say of that. For all I know Ambrosi – Syngva – still sleeps in the Iron Ash and will sleep there for ever.

The Iron Ash grows in the Ghost World: its roots go down into chaos, and it spreads its iron leaves among the stars. Our world, and all other worlds, are clouds caught in its branches; and its sleepers are the sleepers who dream us.

And that is the end of this story (says the cat) and the beginning of another. If it was not true, then neither do I walk around this tree.

If you thought this story tasty, then serve it to others (says the cat).
If you thought it sour, then sweeten it with your own telling.
But whether you liked it or not, take it away and let it make its own way back to me, riding on another's tongue.

The cat lays herself down among the links of her golden chain and tucks her forepaws beneath her breast. Head up, ears pricked, she falls asleep under her oak-tree, and neither sings nor tells stories.